MYTHOLOGY OF THE

NORTH AMERICAN INDIAN AND INUIT NATIONS

MYTHOLOGY OF THE
NORTH AMERICAN
INDIAN AND
INUIT NATIONS

MYTHS AND LEGENDS OF NORTH AMERICA

BRIAN L
MOLYNEAUX

southwater

For my mother, Mary, in memory of my father, Fred, and for my own family: Wendy and our children Fred, Alexandra and Lily.

This edition is published by Southwater

Southwater is an imprint of Anness Publishing Ltd
Hermes House, 88–89 Blackfriars Road, London SE1 8HA
tel. 020 7401 2077; fax 020 7633 9499

www.southwaterbooks.com; www.annesspublishing.com

Anness Publishing has a new picture agency outlet for publishing, promotions or advertising, please visit our website www.practicalpictures.com for more information.

© Anness Publishing Ltd 2003, 2006

UK agent: The Manning Partnership Ltd,
6 The Old Dairy, Melcombe Road, Bath BA2 3LR;
tel. 01225 478444; fax 01225 478440;
sales@manning-partnership.co.uk

UK distributor: Grantham Book Services Ltd,
Isaac Newton Way, Alma Park Industrial Estate,
Grantham, Lincs NG31 9SD; tel. 01476 541080;
fax 01476 541061; orders@gbs.tbs-ltd.co.uk

North American agent/distributor: National Book Network,
4501 Forbes Boulevard, Suite 200, Lanham, MD 20706;
tel. 301 459 3366; fax 301 429 5746; www.nbnbooks.com

Australian agent/distributor: Pan Macmillan Australia,
Level 18, St Martins Tower, 31 Market St, Sydney,
NSW 2000; tel. 1300 135 113; fax 1300 135 103;
customer.service@macmillan.com.au

New Zealand agent/distributor: David Bateman Ltd,
30 Tarndale Grove, Off Bush Road, Albany, Auckland;
tel. (09) 415 7664; fax (09) 415 8892

A CIP catalogue record for this book is available from the British Library.

Publisher: Joanna Lorenz
Managing Editor: Helen Sudell
Project Editor: Sue Barraclough
Design: Mario Bettella, Artmedia
Map Illustrator: Stephen Sweet
Picture Researchers: Veneta Bullen (UK),
    Anita Dickhuth (US)
Editorial Reader: Richard McGinlay
Production Controller: Nick Thompson

10 9 8 7 6 5 4 3 2 1

Page 1: *DANCERS ON THE NORTHWEST COAST OF NORTH AMERICA*
Frontispiece: *DEVIL'S TOWER, WYOMING*
Title page: *CARVED REPLICA OF A KACHINA GOD CALLED TIHU*
This page: *THUNDERBIRD ON A TOTEM POLE*
Page 8: *MANDAN COMING OF AGE CEREMONY*
Page 16: *PUEBLO CAVES, NEW MEXICO*
Opposite: *A MONSTROUS FLYING HEAD OF BLACKFOOT MYTHOLOGY*

PUBLISHER'S NOTE: The entries in this encyclopedia are all listed alphabetically. Names in italic capital letters indicate the name has an individual entry. Special feature spreads examine specific mythological themes in more detail. If a character or subject is included in a special feature spread it is noted at the end of their individual entry.

CONTENTS

PREFACE

This encyclopedia is a collection of essays, descriptions and accounts of the myths and legends of the continent of North America, from the Canadian Arctic to the northern deserts of Mexico. These are lands of great contrast – frigid tundra, cool and searing deserts, vast grasslands and forests, lush woodlands, humid swamps and immense mountain ranges.

The native peoples are as diverse as these landscapes: hundreds of societies, tribal groups and nations, speaking many different languages, spread across Canada and the United States. Their traditions concerning the origins of life and their place within the natural world, once passed on through story-telling and now written down, reflect ways of life based variously on hunting and gathering, agriculture and fishing.

Humans probably entered America when it was joined to Asia by an Ice Age land bridge and the North Atlantic was ice-bound. The first peoples were nomads: gathering, fishing and hunting in seasonal rounds.They moved southward gradually, following the ice-free coasts and moving up rivers into the interior. By 9000 BC they had reached the tip of South America.

By about 5000 BC, people had discovered how to cultivate a variety of the plants they gathered and how to domesticate some of the animals around them. Tending these plants and animals involved settling in one place; then – as trade in surplus food began to develop in the ensuing millennia – villages were able to support specialist craftsmen who produced objects and provided services over and above the barest necessities of life. Some societies became yet more complex, and towns developed, with powerful rulers and organized priesthoods.

DANCE was an important part of ritual for many tribal peoples, and invariably had both a spiritual and practical significance. These dancers are assuming the spirit of the bear, giving them the power and wisdom necessary for successful hunting.

However, most of these cultures did not evolve steadily from nomad groups to townsfolk, or abandon their natural spirituality, focused on earth and sky, for great corporate religions intertwined with the power structures of a nation. In some environments – too harsh, remote, impenetrable or infertile to support the denser populations from which complex societies could develop – the inhabitants continued to gather, fish and hunt, or work small garden plots near their camps or villages, or tend animals. And some complex societies developed too far – collapsing as they exhausted the environment that had sustained them – while others fell victim to climatic change or natural disaster, or were conquered by neighbouring tribes.

Yet each of these diverse cultures had one thing in common: the need for a philosophy that would explain not only the vastness and power of the cosmos and the wonders of nature, but also the mysteries of the human mind, with its desires, its fears and its capacities for good and evil, creation and destruction, and selfishness and altruism. This philosophy, captured in myths and legends, enabled these different cultures to find meaning, balance and a sense of place in the world they inherited.

Mythology is not just a miscellaneous collection of old tales; it embraces all of what we now call religion, science and philosophy (natural, moral and metaphysical). It asks fundamental questions – how the world began, how it will end, where humans fit in and how they can influence it, and how individuals and communities should interact. Since the questions are the same, we see common threads running through the myths and legends described here: heavens above and nether worlds below; the critical importance of the sun, moon and stars; gods, heroes and monsters creating, transforming and destroying successions of nascent worlds; and the sacred significance of the landscape itself, and of particular elements within it. Legends bring the sacred essence of the world into the great sweep of history by interpreting the exploits of real-life heroes and earth-shattering events within a spiritual context. In this way, the entire course of life resonates with the core beliefs of the society.

Even as the myths and legends of North America share a common sense of spirituality, answers to the questions of life vary with the societies that ask them. The Choctaw ancestors, emerging out of the hill of Nanih Waiya (in present day Mississippi) from their previous world, looked out on a landscape very different from the one that greeted the first Hopi who climbed through an opening into the Grand Canyon of Arizona and the Makah who found themselves in a vast plain of sand and grass, surrounded by animal people. In the fertile Mississippi Valley, the Choctaw became agriculturalists who shared many religious features with their Mesoamerican cousins, such as sun worship, raised earthen ceremonial plazas, burial mounds, and artistic and religious symbols; the Hopi wandered across their world until they found a home in the semi-desert lands of northeastern Arizona, where they developed corn (maize) horticulture to a level of biological and cultural sophistication unrivalled today; and the Makah, like their relatives along the northern Pacific coast, became skilled seafarers, hunting whales and other sea mammals. However, similar myths can appear in the most diverse societies and environments: the "bird nester" theme (one of two competitors persuades his rival to make a perilous climb to gather birds' eggs, then removes the ladder to maroon him). This myth is found among the Yurok of the Californian coast, and also appears far to the south in a Brazilian rainforest culture. Note too, the prominence of serpents in religious imagery or the popularity of the tricksters Coyote and Raven among many North American peoples. It is these contrasting threads of similarity and difference, confirmation and contradiction, and the search for basic truths, that make the fabric of the mythology of North America so fascinating.

OLD BEAR was a Mandan shaman. The shaman's influence lay in his spiritual powers and knowledge of ceremony. (PAINTING BY GEORGE CATLIN, 1832)

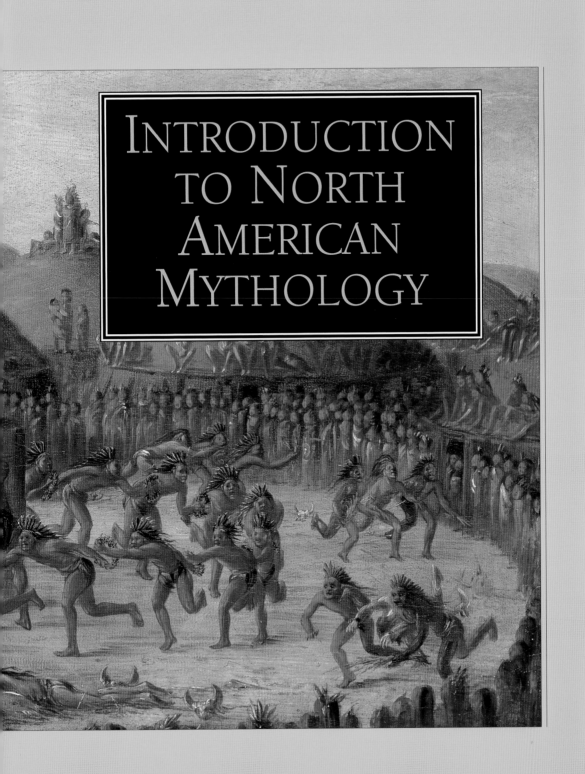

INTRODUCTION TO NORTH AMERICAN MYTHOLOGY

INTRODUCTION

THE CULTURAL HERITAGE of North American aboriginal peoples includes oral traditions remembered and preserved in mythologies. Story-tellers over thousands of years of Native North American culture have been unconstrained by literary form, which can transform inspiration into rigid canons of belief and practice. They have been free to listen to their own heritage and speak with voices that reflect individual vision and the wisdom of the ages. Personal insight, sought through dreams, vision quests and other forms of inspiration, is a critical aspect of spirituality in most North American aboriginal cultures. It makes the mythology as mutable – and fragile – as the story-teller's world. Yet, by living in the spoken word, the song and the dance, the spirits of the imagination survive across generations, passing on the essence of what it takes to be a human being.

The Spiritual Life

People of all cultures define the world as they experience it, so their mythologies must account for what they see. Every part of a landscape has the potential for spiritual identity. This is often literal: high places are close to the sky and the remote gods; caves provide entry into the earth and its hidden spiritual forces. Other, less dramatic, places and objects involved in mythological events only have meaning if a narrative survives. All material things have spiritual potential – from tiny stones worn down in birds' gizzards, kept by some tribes as powerful medicine, to the great trees used to construct ceremonial lodges. Moreover, in many cultures, every living thing harks back to a time when all creatures spoke with a common voice and pursued similar social lives. This mythological age is not lost in the deep past defined by science, for aboriginal concepts of time are both linear and cyclical: linear as the steps and stages of a human life, and cyclical as the generations that renew all life and the

earth itself. This endless spiral means that the past never recedes into the distance; even the time of creation is only just beyond the reach of the story-teller. The mythological narratives of a culture are thus an eternal present, renewing social identity with every telling.

Native North Americans once shared the most ancient of patterns of life – moving from place to place, following the seasonal shifts of nature to gather wild plants and hunt game – and the religious beliefs and mythologies of hunters and gatherers reflect this. Their search for spiritual knowledge and understanding was seen in terms of a journey, a quest for vision, that took them away from the protection of their familiar surroundings into a natural world containing the mysterious forces that brought life and death, famine and plenty.

When many centuries of harvesting native plant species gradually developed into a formalized agriculture – sparked by the spread of corn (maize) from Mexico well over 2,000 years ago – some peoples adopted a more sedentary life. These horticultural groups adapted their belief systems to the rhythms of lives spent in one place and measured by the structured routines

of planting, tending and harvesting corn (maize), beans, squash and other crops in gardens and fields. Unlike nomadic hunters and gatherers – who, through personal quests or with the help of shamans, gained access to the spirits wherever they moved – farming people most often focused their worlds in the ceremonial centres of their villages, enclosed by a familiar landscape, and tended to develop organized priesthoods and religions.

The European Invasion

Immediately after the first contact with Europeans in the 17th century, the introduction of their trade goods and domesticated animals to cultures reliant on natural substances – such as stone, bone, plant fibres and clays – had a dramatic impact on North American cultures.

DEVIL'S TOWER, Wyoming, known to the Lakota as Mato Tipila, has drawn people to it for at least 10,000 years. It figures in the mythologies of the Arapaho, Cheyenne, Kiowa, Sioux and other regional tribes. In ancient times, the great mass of volcanic rock provided shelter for practical and spiritual needs, and gave hunters excellent views across the Belle Fourche Valley. Its rock-strewn flanks are now important sites for vision quests and other personal rituals, while the surrounding grasslands are the settings for Sun Dances and other significant tribal ceremonies.

CEREMONIES forge the link between the land, human life, and the creative and nurturing powers of nature. In this representation by a Zia Pueblo artist of a mythical corn ceremony, the broad leaves of the plant shelter drummers who sing sacred songs while dancers, under the life-giving rain, offer gifts to the creative essence above the sky. (PAINTING BY IGNACIO MOQUINO, 1938.)

Horses, metal, glass, firearms – all seemed at first magical and then essential, disrupting cultural routines that had taken centuries to develop. When white soldiers, missionaries, traders and settlers followed, they set in motion what was to become a devastating and irreversible process of social disintegration that had a disastrous effect on tradition. Except for those in the remotest forest regions of the north and in the Arctic, almost all tribes were decimated or eliminated by force of arms or disease, and distracted from their traditional hunting-and-gathering or farming economies by the fur trade and the lure of European material goods that it brought. By the mid-19th century they had been driven from their homelands to distant reservations. These new lands were generally infertile, rugged and remote, with little perceived economic potential to Europeans. Yet hunter-gatherers were expected to take up farming, and farmers were meant to raise crops, on the poor, often arid, soils. On many reservations, individual tribes were forced to cohabit with others, speaking different languages and following different traditions. They were assaulted by governments intent on destroying indigenous culture through Western education, the substitution of English for native tongues, and indoctrination in Christianity – which included systematic attempts to eliminate ancient religions.

The cultural dissonance was intense because native people held concepts of land use and property, of time, of the nature of the world itself, that were dramatically different from those of white people. When Sauk and Fox chiefs, plied with lavish gifts and liquor, signed away their lands in the Treaty of 1804 for a meagre sum of money, the great Sauk chief Black Hawk explained his actions thus: "My reason teaches me that land cannot be sold. The Great Spirit gave it to his children to live upon. So long as they occupy and cultivate it they have the right to the soil. Nothing can be sold but such things as can be carried away." Only on the Northwest Coast, where families and clans held rights to virtually all aspects of life, from myths to shellfish beds, and among some northern Californian tribes, did hunters and gatherers regard land as property. The absolute loss of land was inconceivable to most chiefs, even when they actually signed it away. American Indians were also baffled by Western concepts of time. The rigorous segmentation of life into equal fragments imposed a strange and different rhythm, one that responded to mathematical logic rather than reflecting the changing patterns of nature.

The American Indians drew their identity from the intertwining of the natural world around them and the spiritual world that was their philosophy, science and religion. From the reservations, the view of the spiritual and

THE MISSION was a familiar sight in Southern California by the early 19th century. Starting at San Diego in 1789, Franciscan friars founded 21 missions along El Camino Real ("the Royal Road") to Sonoma, in order to bring Christianity to the region's native tribes. The techniques of the missionaries were both subtle and aggressive, leading many people to question the wisdom of their own spirituality. This view of San Gabriel Mission, near present-day Los Angeles, shows an American Indian dwelling in the foreground. (PAINTING BY FERDINAND DEPPE, 1832.)

physical world was not the same as it had once been. Traditional sacred sites and landscapes – the very foundations of tribal culture – were no longer accessible, because they were on white-controlled private land. Many elders, the keepers of traditional knowledge, were among the staggering numbers that died following the move to reservations. Others lost touch with ancestral roots as a result of the pressures of assimilation, and many younger people were unable to maintain their cultural identities. By the mid-20th century, mythologies, and the narratives and rituals that made them vital, reflected this dissolution of cultural integrity, surviving in many places as half-remembered fragments, or disappearing altogether.

There were some groups among whom the strong core of native beliefs persisted. Some occupied lands unattractive to whites, such as the Arctic and Subarctic, interior mountain regions and the deserts of the Southwest. Some maintained a relatively independent economy, including a few of the seagoing cultures of the Northwest Coast. Others retained significant land bases within their traditional homelands. Ultimately, as environmental awareness began to strengthen in the second half of the 20th century, aboriginal philosophies of respect for,

and sensitivity to, the earth and its resources rose to prominence. In this atmosphere of new-found respect, mythologies were no longer the quaint stories of disappearing cultures, but ideas and beliefs that made a direct connection between human life and the surrounding world. The depredations of 400 years of domination by Western culture had left an indelible mark; nonetheless, the new relevance of these ancient mythologies inspired spiritual regeneration, rediscovery and re-creation of the knowledge that was almost lost. The growing cultural strength of North America's first nations continues to this day, with new narrative forms – literature, theatre and electronic media – growing beside the traditional arts of story-telling, visual arts, drama and dance. These new visions look forward, at the same time respecting tradition and recalling the lessons of the past. They express, as the ancient elders did, the realities of the present for the sake of the future.

Mythology Today

With such a dramatic and complex background, North American mythology is not easily organized or presented. The individual nature of American Indian religions, the generations of story-tellers, and the difficulty of using one

language to explain another's vision, as well as the loss of traditional culture by assimilation, and the sparse, fragmented collection of oral traditions that remain, all mean that the names (and spellings) and exploits of mythological beings may be highly variable. We draw from many different kinds of sources: anthropological texts, collections of myths, and contemporary Indian narratives. We use traditional names for some characters, and their English translations for others – sometimes the traditional name is already well-known, and sometimes the English name provides a description that would be obscured if the native word was used. The naming of tribes is equally complex. Many tribes were given their names by whites, either because they did not know the tribe's own name for itself or because it did not anglicize easily. Sometimes these names were actually pejoratives used by rivals or enemies. Other tribes never had, or used, a collective name until anthropologists or other whites gave them one. In recent times, some tribes have demanded that their chosen names be used in place of the ones conferred on them by others – the Inuit, for example, rejecting the universally familiar term "Eskimo". In this book we use the names most commonly recognized, while adding variant spellings and the names that tribes may prefer themselves in parentheses or, if the new name is gaining acceptance, in the main text.

Given the significance of the natural environment to cultural adaptation and expression, we divide tribal groups according to the regions in which they last lived freely: the Arctic, the Subarctic (northern, or boreal, forests), the Northeast, the Southeast, the Great Plains, the Southwest, California, the Great Basin, the Columbia Plateau, and the Northwest Coast. The distinct environmental character of each of these regions strongly influenced its peoples, determining, for example, whether an individual group had the potential to amass food resources or move from hunting and gathering to horticulture and, thus, the pattern of beliefs that would develop within the group as a result.

Environment, and the proximity of tribes to each other, has a much greater influence on the form a culture takes than language does, but knowledge of the language of one's traditions is crucial to cultural identity. Language also gives us an understanding of tribal origins and relationships, for the languages that exist today all developed over thousands of years from roots in Asia. Languages change and diversify over time, especially if the population is highly dispersed and isolated. However, through identifying similar words and grammatical constructions used by different groups, linguists can identify many language-family relationships although a few languages defy analysis, perhaps because their origins lie so deep in the past that the shared words and grammatical constructions are now obscure.

The study of North American native languages shows that tribal groups within a language family tend to cluster in certain regions – the Algonquian peoples in the northern part of the continent, and the Uto-Aztecan peoples in the south, for instance – but there are also outlying groups speaking a language unrelated to those of the cultures around them. Since language relationships may persist in spite of dramatic changes in a culture, anomalies in the distribution of languages may reveal evidence of ancient migrations. Perhaps the most dramatic example in North America is the Navajo. These herders and farmers of the Southwest region are identified with sand paintings and a complex mythology focused on corn. Yet they speak an Athapascan language related to the languages of groups living as far north as Alaska and the Northwest Territories, who spend their lives hunting and fishing in the northern forests.

North American mythologies were once as diverse as the languages and environments of its original inhabitants.

CHILDREN offer the best chance to keep alive the spirit of a culture. Among Indian peoples, the interaction between elders and the very young provides the spiritual strength that young people need as they grow. The Navajo children gathered here listen to an elder, whose stories of history, legendary heroes and the events of creation ensure that future generations keep their cultural identity through the dramatic changes they will experience in their lifetimes.

But in our modern "information society", native voices often speak of a common reality: putting the case that individual groups must work together to achieve the strength they need to regain lost rights and lost lands. This is reflected in a spread of common religions, common rituals and common mythologies among once diverse tribes. Nevertheless, the vitality of surviving mythologies teaches that there is also strength in diversity. By keeping the link between peoples and their homelands, a wealth of unique cultural heritage can flourish, and its narratives carry the life experiences and wisdom of thousands of generations into the future.

The past 400 years in North America are a history of cultural and linguistic decline and extinction. Now the challenges to native cultures include the revival of tradition and the renewal of mythology to accommodate new political and social realities.

THE CREATIVE ARTS are flourishing today, reflecting a renewal of pride among aboriginal peoples. Cedar woodcarving along the Northwest Coast carries on a tradition extending several thousand years into the past, but with a new freedom, generated by a changing society and access to new technologies. In a modern depiction of the Haida origin story, the formal symmetry of the traditional style gives way to a more dynamic expression (left), as Raven opens the clam shell and releases the first humans on to the muddy flats left by receding primordial waters. (CEDAR CARVING BY BILL REID.)

LANGUAGES OF THE TRIBES

A language is not merely a way of speaking: it is a way of seeing and explaining the world. English translations of stories told in native tongues can only reveal the surface of the deep emotional and philosophical insights that the original words embodied. Even so, such translations give us an opening into an intellectual world that extends back thousands of years. Although we cannot *hear* the words in which these stories were first spoken, study of the languages reveals subtle relationships among the tribes of the North American aboriginal family that help to account for the sharing of mythological characters, events and themes.

This study, which explores the development of languages by tracing them back to common roots, is highly complex. the thousands of languages and dialects spoken during prehistoric times are now a few hundred, many of which are on the verge of extinction, so

that linguists have little to work with. Classification is therefore always hypothetical and, since research continues, in a state of flux.

This table provides a very general organization of languages and dialects spoken by the people of the tribes mentioned. Some language phyla and families and many languages and dialects are therefore left out. The left column contains the language family name under which all related languages are grouped, and each succeeding column to the right represents a more detailed group, subgroup, language or dialect. Isolate languages are those thought to be unconnected to any other group. As languages develop and diversify over time, the left-to-right shift is also (putatively) a shift in time, from past to present, across the centuries of aboriginal life in North America. Since the classification is intended as a rough sketch, we have omitted more detailed language relationships at

the tribal level, as many of these are still subject to scholarly debate.

Readers who wish to pursue this fascinating subject further may consult the sources used for the following scheme:

Joseph E. Grimes and Barbara F. Grimes (eds), *Ethnologue Language Family Index* (13th ed.), Dallas TX: Summer Institute of Linguistics, 1996 (also see www.sil.org/ethnologue/families).

Alvin M. Josephy, jr. (ed.), *America in 1492*, New York: Vintage Books, 1993.

Carl Waldman, *Atlas of the North American Indian*, New York: Facts on File, 1985.

The *Ethnologue* classification, which is generally adhered to here, follows the classification scheme of William O. Bright (ed.), *International Encyclopedia of Linguistics*, Oxford and New York: Oxford University Press, 1992.

LANGUAGE FAMILIES

Language subgroup(s):
  Language/dialect name Tribe name

ALGIC:
  Algonquian:
    Central:
      Cree (5 dialects)   Cree
      Kickapoo   Kickapoo
      Menominee   Menominee
      Mesquaki   Fox
      Montagnais   Montagnais
      Ojibwa (4 dialects)   Ojibwa
      Potawatomi   Potawatomi
    Eastern:
      Abnaki-Penobscot   Abenaki, Penobscot
      Delaware   Delaware
      Maliseet-Passamaquoddy
                         Malecite-Passamaquoddy
      Micmac   Micmac
      Naskapi   Naskapi
    Plains:
      Arapaho   Arapaho
      Blackfoot   Blackfoot
      Cheyenne   Cheyenne
      Gros Ventre   Gros Ventre
      Wiyot isolate   Wiyot
      Yurok isolate   Yurok

CADDOAN
  Northern:
      Arikara   Arikara
      Pawnee   Pawnee
      Wichita   Wichita

ESKIMO-ALEUT
      Aleut   Aleut
      Inuit   Inuit

HOKAN
  Esselen-Yuman:
      Mohave   Mojave
  Northern:
      Karok   Karuk
  Salinan-Seri:
      Chumash   Chumash

IROQUOIAN
  Northern:
      Cayuga   Cayuga
      Mohawk   Mohawk
      Oneida   Oneida
      Onondaga   Onondaga
      Seneca   Seneca
      Tuscarora   Tuscarora
      Wyandot   Wyandot
  Southern:
      Cherokee   Cherokee

KERESCAN
      Cochiti   Cochiti Pueblo
      Keres   Keres Pueblo

KIOWA-TANOAN
  Kiowa-Towa:
      Jemez   Towa Pueblo
      Kiowa   Kiowa
  Tewa-Tiwa:
      Tewa   Tewa Pueblo
      Tiwa (northern and southern)
                               Tiwa Pueblo

KUTENAI isolate   Kootenay

MUSKOGEAN
  Eastern:
      Alabama   Alabama
      Muskogee   Creek, Tuskegee
      Seminole   Seminole
  Western:
      Choctaw   Choctaw

NA-DENE
  Athapascan:
  Apachean:
      Jicarilla Apache   Jicarilla Apache
      Kiowa Apache   Kiowa Apache
      Lipan Apache   Lipan Apache
      Mescalero-Chiricahua Apache
                        Mescalero-Chiricahua Apache
      Navajo   Navajo
      Western Apache   Aravaipa Apache
  Canadian:
      Beaver   Beaver
      Chipewyan   Chipewyan
      Dogrib   Dogrib
      Han   Han
      Hare   Sahtu
      Sarsi   Sarcee
      Slavey   Slavey
      Yellowknife   Yellowknife
  Ingalik-Koyukon:
      Degexit'an   Degexit'an
      Koyukon   Koyukon
  Pacific Coast:
      Hupa   Hupa
  Tahltan-Kaska:
      Tahltan   Tahltan
  Tanana-Upper Kuskokwim:
      Haida isolate   Haida
      Tanana   Tanana
      Tlingit isolate   Tlingit

PENUTIAN
  California Penutian:
      Maidu (4 dialects)   Maidu
      Miwok (6 dialects)   Miwok, Yosemite
      Wintun   Wintu
  Chinookan:
      Chinook   Chinook
  Plateau Penutian:
      Klamath-Modoc   Klamath, Modoc
      Nez Perce   Nez Perce
      Yakima   Yakima

Tsimshian:
      Nass-Gitksian   Niska, Gitksan
      Tsimshian   Tsimshian
      Zuni isolate (incorporation under Penutian is
      hypothetical)   Zuni

SALISHAN
      Bella Coola   Bella Coola
      Central Salish   Coast Salish
  Interior Salish:
      Flathead-Kalispel   Flathead
      Okanagan   Okanagan
      Sanpoil   Sanpoil
      Colville   Colville
  Tsamosan:
      Lower Chehalis   Lower Chehalis
      Upper Chehalis   Upper Chehalis

SIOUAN
  Central:
      Assiniboine   Assiniboine
      Dakota   Mdewakanton,
                               Wahpekute, Sisseton
                               and Wahpeton
      Iowa-Oto   Iowa
      Lakota   Teton
      Mandan   Mandan
      Nakota   Yankton, Yanktonai
      Omaha-Ponca   Omaha
      Quapaw   Quapaw
      Stoney   Stoney
      Winnebago   Winnebago
  Missouri Valley:
      Crow   Crow
      Hidatsa   Hidatsa

UTO-AZTECAN
  Northern:
      Comanche   Comanche
      Hopi   Hopi
      Luiseño   Luiseño
      Northern Paiute   Northern Paiute
      Serrano   Gabrielino
      Shoshoni   Shoshoni
      Ute-Southern Paiute   Ute, Southern Paiute
  Southern:
      Papago-Pima   Papago, Pima

WAKASHAN
  Northern:
      Kwakiutl   Kwakiutl
  Southern:
      Makah   Makah
      Nootka   Nootka

YUKI
      Wappo   Wappo
      Yuki   Yuki

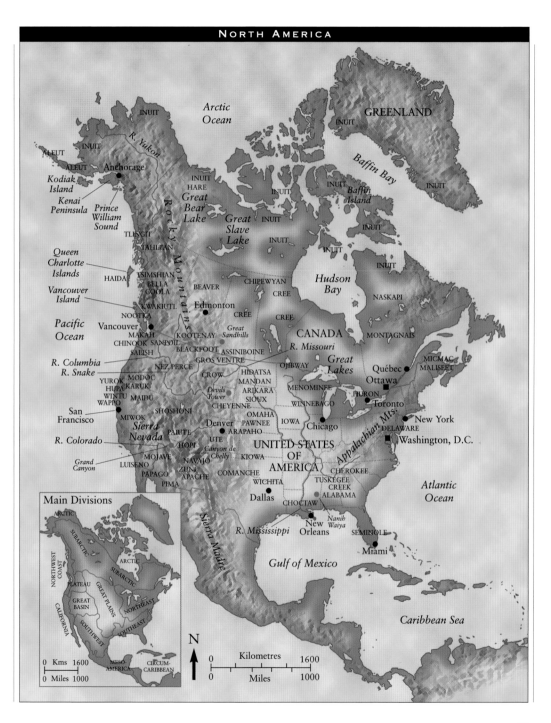

NORTH AMERICA

Arctic Ocean

GREENLAND

INUIT

INUIT

Baffin Bay

ALEUT
INUIT
ALEUT
Anchorage
INUIT
HARE
Great Bear Lake
INUIT
INUIT
Baffin Island
INUIT

Kodiak Island
Kenai Peninsula
Prince William Sound

Great Slave Lake
INUIT
INUIT

TLINGIT
TAHLTAN

INUIT

INUIT

Queen Charlotte Islands

Hudson Bay

TSIMSHIAN
BELLA COOLA
CHIPEWYAN
CREE
NASKAPI

HAIDA
BEAVER

Vancouver Island

KWAKIUTL
Edmonton
CREE
CREE
MONTAGNAIS

NOOTKA
Great Sandhills

Pacific Ocean
Vancouver
KOOTENAY
CANADA

MAKAH
CHINOOK SANPOIL
BLACKFOOT
ASSINIBOINE
R. Missouri
MICMAC
MALISEET

SALISH
GROS VENTRE
Great Lakes
Québec

R. Columbia
R. Snake
NEZ PERCE
CROW
OJIBWAY
Ottawa

YUROK MODOC
HIDATSA
MANDAN
MENOMINEE
HURON

KARUK
HUPA
WINTU MAIDU
ARIKARA
SIOUX
WINNEBAGO
Toronto

WAPPO
SHOSHONI
CHEYENNE

San Francisco
MIWOK
Sierra Nevada
PAIUTE
OMAHA
PAWNEE
IOWA
Chicago
New York

R. Colorado
HOPI
UTE
ARAPAHO
DELAWARE
Washington, D.C.

Canyon de Chelly

Grand Canyon
MOJAVE
LUISENO
NAVAJO
ZUNI
APACHE
KIOWA
UNITED STATES OF AMERICA
Appalachian Mts.

PAPAGO
PIMA
COMANCHE
WICHITA
CHEROKEE

Atlantic Ocean

TUSKEGEE
CREEK
ALABAMA

Dallas
CHOCTAW

New Orleans
Nanih Waiya
SEMINOLE

R. Mississippi

Sierra Madre

Miami

Gulf of Mexico

Caribbean Sea

Main Divisions

ARCTIC
SUBARCTIC
NORTHWEST COAST
ARCTIC
SUBARCTIC
PLATEAU
GREAT PLAINS
GREAT BASIN
CALIFORNIA
NORTHEAST
SOUTHWEST
SOUTHEAST
MESO-AMERICA
CIRCUM-CARIBBEAN

0 Kms 1600
0 Miles 1000

N

0 Kilometres 1600
0 Miles 1000

15

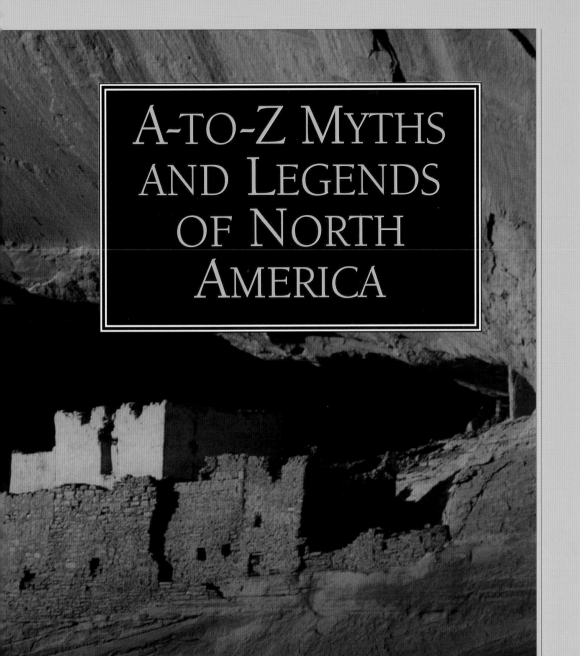

A-TO-Z MYTHS
AND LEGENDS
OF NORTH
AMERICA

A

THE ABENAKI (Abnaki) is a group of Algonquian-speaking tribes who ranged throughout the Atlantic maritime regions of southern Canada and the northeastern United States. The centre of their traditional homeland was present-day Maine, where the eastern Abenaki (including the *PENOBSCOT*, the *PASSAMAQUODDY*, and the *MALISEET*) hunted moose, deer and other game, fished the many lakes and rivers, and gathered wild plants. The western Abenaki, who occupied the milder inlands across Vermont and New Hampshire to the eastern shores of Lake Champlain in New York, subsisted mainly by horticulture and fishing.

The wars of the 18th century, which prompted the Abenaki and *MICMAC* to form the *WABANAKI* confederacy, forced many Abenaki to flee into Quebec, where they continue to live today. The rest occupy reservations in northern Maine (Penobscot, Passamaquoddy and Maliseet) and reserves in New Brunswick (Maliseet) or are scattered across the non-Indian lands and communities of the region.

THE AFTERLIFE

THE AFTERLIFE is, for most peoples, a journey to the land of the dead, a place of spiritual repose and comfort, if not happiness.

For the *INUIT*, the Land of the Dead lies above the sky. The sky itself is solid, pierced by holes that let in light and sometimes spill celestial fluids that fall as snow or rain into the land of the living. Above the sky the ghosts of the dead may find rest, for the air is warm, the sky is bright, and land animals are abundant. As if in reaction against the often hard life by the ocean, only a few variants of the Inuit myth mention seals, walruses and other sea creatures.

Sometimes, the desire to prolong the familiar in the afterlife reflects the harsher realities of life in the recent past. The Chiricahua *APACHE* people believe that the dead fall through a trapdoor

AN INUIT MOON MASK from western Alaska. The board around the face represents air, the hoops symbolize levels of the cosmos, and the feathers are stars. Inuit believe that the souls of the dead first rise into the heavens. After regaining their spiritual energy they travel with the moon down to earth again, where they may take human or animal form.

hidden by tall grass and slide down a great mountain of sand to the underworld. This world is similar to the Apache's own, extending, in one account, to the presence of white people.

AH-AH-NEE-NIN

see *GROS VENTRE*.

THE ALABAMA

THE ALABAMA people lived originally in what is now Alabama and Mississippi, growing corn (maize), beans and other crops in the warm, fertile river valleys, and hunting and gathering when necessary. They are close relatives of the Coushatta, who speak a similar Muskogean language. The two nations fragmented during the European conquest and were uprooted in the 19th century, when the United States government forcibly removed all southeastern tribes to Oklahoma. Just three small groups have survived: the Coushattas of Louisiana, the Alabama-Coushatta Tribe of Polk County, Texas, and the Alabamas and Quassartes of Oklahoma.

THE ALEUT

THE ALEUT consist of several Arctic cultures occupying the north Pacific and Bering Sea regions between North America and Asia. The Alutiiq inhabit the coastal areas of south-central Alaska, including Prince William Sound, Kodiak Island (which has the largest concentration of villages) and the Kenai and Alaska Peninsulas. The Aleut peoples of the western Aleutian Islands and the Commander Islands (Russia) have a distinctive language and culture. All Aleuts resemble the *INUIT* in their way of life, exploiting the abundant resources of land and sea (especially sea mammals, such as otters, and caribou). They lived in semi-subterranean houses, built of timbers and banked with earth. The effects of the trade in sea-otter fur and sealskin, beginning with Russian exploitation in the 19th century, were devastating, but the Aleuts' survival was ensured by their fierce resistance by their remoteness from centres of white American culture, and by the 20th-century decline in the fur trade.

ALINNAQ

see *MOON MAN*.

ALWAYS-LIVING-AT-THE-COAST

ALWAYS-LIVING-AT-THE-COAST (*KWAKIUTL*) became the progenitor of killer whales after a dramatic encounter with *COYOTE*.

Always-Living-at-the-Coast had a notoriously unmarried daughter named Death-Bringing Woman. She had received many suitors, but their reward had been death, and their bones were piled high. Coyote decided to paddle his canoe down to the coast to court her. Some people along the way mocked his effort, and he transformed them into birds and then into the first deer; others encouraged him, so he created rich salmon and shellfish grounds on the spot. Then, a young woman whose sight he restored told him Death-Bringing Woman's terrible secret: she had a toothed vagina. She gave him a stone chisel and instructed him to blunt the teeth when the time came. Coyote did, and, with her weapons gone, Death-Bringing Woman happily accepted him as her husband. Angered, her father Always-Living-at-the-Coast tried several times to kill Coyote, but he always failed.

One day Coyote and his wife joined the old man in his canoe. As they paddled across the sea, Coyote chewed a piece of wood until it was soft, formed it into the shape of a killer whale and threw it into the water, exclaiming that the old man would be the killer whale of future generations. At that moment, whales rose out of the sea and dragged Always-Living-at-the-Coast under the waves.

THE ALASKAN SEA OTTER (Enhydra lutris lutris), *was hunted to near extinction in the 18th and 19th centuries because of its luxurious fur. It is once again thriving.*

ANISHINABE see *OJIBWAY*.

THE APACHE [Jicarilla, *KIOWA*, Lipan, Mescalero-Chiricahua, Aravaipa] speak an Athapascan language. As the Athapascan home-land is the Subarctic, it is clear that the Apache migrated from these northern regions to their present homelands in the southwestern United States and in northern Mexico. They put their hunting and gathering skills to good use in the rugged southwestern landscapes and, where appropriate, took up farming and herding. Five main tribal groups exist today: the Jicarilla Apache, Kiowa Apache, Lipan Apache, Mescalero-Chiricahua Apache and Aravaipa (Western) Apache. The Kiowa Apache, during the original migration, joined up with and were influenced by the Kiowa, an unrelated people moving south from the mountainous regions of the upper Missouri who spoke a Kiowa-Tanoan language. They eventually settled in the southern Great Plains, south of the Kiowa proper, and now live in Oklahoma. The Chiricahua people, also known as the Fort Sill Apache Tribe, live mostly in Apache, Oklahoma; the Jicarilla people live in northern New Mexico; and the Lipan live with the Mescalero and a group of Chiricahua people on the

SHARP NOSE was a great Arapaho leader. Facing the destruction of his people, he travelled to Washington, DC, in 1877 with two other Shoshoni leaders, Black Coal and Friday, and negotiated successfully for the establishment of an Arapaho reservation.

Mescalero Reservation in New Mexico. The Aravaipa occupy lands in central southern Arizona.

APOONIVI (*HOPI*) is a prominent rise with a whiteish top that lies southwest of the Oraibi mesa (plateau), one of the major Hopi settlements in northeastern Arizona. When a person dies, his or her spirit climbs steps up the slope of this hill on its way to Maski, the Home of the Dead.

THE ARAPAHO [Northern, Southern] originated as one of the Algonquian-speaking peoples of the Great Lakes region. Some time in the last few thousand years they migrated to the Great Plains to pursue a life of nomadic buffalo-hunting. They once occupied territories from southeastern Wyoming, through southwestern Nebraska and eastern Colorado, to northwestern Kansas.

The Northern Arapaho live on the Wind River Reservation in Wyoming, and the Southern Arapaho are scattered all across

non-reservation land allotments throughout Oklahoma.

ARCHITECTURE, in the form of shelters, is often conceived as a microcosm of the supernaturally created earth and its sheltering sky.

In a Skidi *PAWNEE* account of the origin of the earthlodge, *TIRÁWAHAT*, the creator, planned the structure to take care of earth children born of stars. From their place in the sky, each of the star gods put a post in the ground, and Tiráwahat marked his own place in the centre with an ash tree. The *LODGE* opened to the east – the direction of warmth and light, thought and planning – and up to the sky. The Chief's Council (the constellation Corona Borealis) got the Sun to send down fire to burn the tree. It became the first hearth,

APACHE HEADWARE depicting a meteor or shooting star. It may represent a powerful, protective spirit perceived in a dream.

and, from this time on, its coals got their light from the Morning Star and the Sun. As the smoke-hole faced the sky, the abode of the creator and the source of all wisdom and instruction, smoke became the carrier of messages to the gods.

THE ARIKARA were Caddoan-speaking horticulturalists and buffalo hunters who lived along the Missouri River in central South Dakota. After falling prey to disease, inter-tribal warfare and other depredations caused by the incursions of white people into the region, they moved with two allied tribes, the *MANDAN* and the *HIDATSA*, into North Dakota. This group, known as the Three Affiliated Tribes, now occupies the Fort Berthold Reservation in North Dakota. They live on the remnants of their land not flooded after the damming of the Missouri in the 1950s.

19

B

ARROW BOY

ARROW BOY (*CHEYENNE*) was a hero who brought the sacred *MEDICINE* bundle ceremonies to his people from the spirit world, ensuring their prosperity. He had an exceptional origin and quickly revealed great supernatural powers.

A woman became pregnant, but four years passed before the child was born. Soon after the birth, his parents died, and the boy went to live with his grandmother. He began to walk and talk almost immediately and, foreshadowing supernatural feats to come, he took his buffalo-calf robe and turned it hair side out, just like a *SHAMAN*. One night, when the shamans gathered to reveal their power, the boy appeared and asked them to cover him with a robe. He then went through an amazing sequence of transformations. The first time the shamans removed the robe, the boy's head was severed; the next time, he was an old man; the next time, a pile of bones; and lastly, he was a boy again. Through these acts, he showed the shamans that he was truly one of them, having mastered the essence of the shamanic process, being able to die and come back to life again.

Since he was still a boy, however, he remained outside the realms of power until a tragic act transformed the lives of his people. He slew a chief, Young Wolf, in a fight over a buffalo he had killed and, when the people learned of this they resolved to kill him, considering him a danger to the tribe. But the boy escaped and, as if by coincidence, all the buffalo disappeared, causing a great famine. Meanwhile, the boy travelled to the high mountains and stumbled upon one with a large opening. When he entered the mountain, he found a council of elders representing each of the tribes. Each man held a sacred bundle – and there was one empty place with a bundle beside it. The elders told him that, if he took this place, he could carry the bundle

back to the Cheyenne and restore their strength. For four years they taught him the bundle ceremony, with its songs and rituals, and revealed the power of the four medicine arrows within the bundle. He also learned how to divine the future and make magic to help in warfare and hunting.

When he returned to his people, he took the name Arrow Boy, as a sign of his spiritual transformation, and he began to exercise his new-found abilities. To ease the famine, he took some buffalo bones and transformed them into fresh meat, and then he began to instruct the people in the proper way to appease the spirits. They camped in a circle and erected a large *TEPEE* in the centre. He called the shamans to bring their rattles and pipes, and, in the shelter of the tepee he sang the four songs of the sacred arrows. As he sang the fourth song, a great roar shook the whole camp – the thundering hooves of a great herd of buffalo! Because Arrow Boy brought the medicine arrows and showed his tribe the way to use them, they never wanted for food again.

THE ASSINIBOINE

THE ASSINIBOINE people are a Siouan tribe that migrated on to the Great Plains from the western Great Lakes region after the introduction of the horse in the 17th century. They occupied a large territory in present-day southern Saskatchewan and adjoining parts of Montana, North Dakota, and Manitoba, following the vast buffalo herds that provided them with

BUFFALO (Bison bison) *roamed the grasslands and forest margins of the Great Plains and Rocky Mountain foothills in vast herds, and were an irresistible lure to hunting and gathering tribes such as the Assiniboine.*

food, clothing and other essentials of daily life. They were historic allies of the *GROS VENTRE*, with whom they now share the Fort Belknap reservation in Montana. Bands also live at the Fort Peck reservation, shared with the *SIOUX*, and several reserves in Canada, including Carry the Kettle and Mosquito Grizzly Bear's Head in Saskatchewan.

AWONAWILONA

AWONAWILONA (*ZUNI*) was an androgynous presence, the "all-container", that created mist out of thoughts when all was dark and empty. As the mist grew thick, it fell as rain and filled the void with a vast ocean, and the creative presence became the Sun. The Sun then took some of its flesh and laid it on the water as a green scum. When it was firm, the mass separated into two great beings, forever locked in an embrace: *MOTHER EARTH* (Awitelin Tsita) and *FATHER SKY* (Apoyan Tachu). These two conceived all life in the four wombs of Awitelin Tsita.

THE BEAR

THE BEAR is a powerful animal that intrigues native thinkers because it is at once fearful of humans, a fierce and dangerous adversary and a shambling beast with speed and great physical agility. Its most curious and significant aspect, however, is that when

it is skinned it looks startlingly human – proof to them of the ancient mythical age when the animal people walked the earth.

In an Eastern *SHOSHONI* account, a man tells of witnessing bears performing a *SUN DANCE*. While on a buffalo hunt, he came upon a trail marked with many bear tracks and followed the tracks to an open place, where he saw the bears gathered around a pine tree. Hiding downwind, so that they would not smell him, he watched the strange ceremony. The pine tree was painted yellow, red and green, and the bears danced in four measured steps forwards and backwards, all the time looking at the pole and singing. Their *puhagant* (*SHAMAN*) had also built a sacred fire. The hunter somehow knew they were praying for the health of their children.

The bear is especially important to the Algonquians of the northern forests. The *MIDEWIWIN* society of the *OJIBWAY* regarded the bear as the most powerful *MANITOU*. When initiates learned the complex songs and rites of the Midé, they were said to follow the bear path in their learning. Among the Eastern

THE GRIZZLY BEAR (Ursus horribilis) *can change from lumbering grace to charging ferocity in a matter of seconds. With its great size and speed, it can easily outrun a human being.*

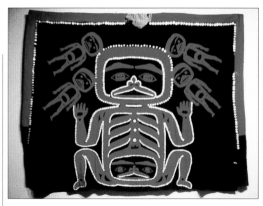

CREE, the master of the bears is Memekwesiw. When shamans conduct divination rites in the small cylindrical or conical structure called a "shaking tent", they sometimes call on him to grant success at hunting. When this great spirit comes into the tent, he fights with the shaman, dragging his massive bear claws against the hide or canvas, clearly visible to those gathered outside. The fight is crucial to the band, for, if the shaman wins, Memekwesiw grants them bears during the next hunt.

To the Lakota SIOUX, the bear has the power to cure, so their shamans seek the help of the bear spirit and use medicinal herbs given their efficacy by it. The HUPA explain how the bear brought them a MEDICINE for controlling complications in pregnancy. Bear got pregnant, but she got so big she had problems walking. As she sat troubled, she was startled by a voice behind her. It was the voice of a redwood sorrel plant, and it told her to pick and eat it. She did, and the next day she was able to walk again. She knew the humans to come would have the same problem, so she decided to pass the medicine on. She imbued the herb with her power so that people could talk to her through it.

The bear is also rightly portrayed as dangerous by American Indian story-tellers. The ALEUT have a moralistic tale of a white-faced bear that was once a man. He was a good hunter who became a bear with white face and feet because he was too successful (a hunter must be prudent when taking game; taking too much is a sign of greed). When other hunters submit to their own greed and try to kill him, he chases them back to their village and tears them apart. The OJIBWAY believe that some powerful shamans court evil by transforming themselves into bears and stalking humans in the night – they are called bear-walkers. (See also SPIRITS OF THE EARTH)

BEAR MOTHER is depicted on a modern Haida button blanket. The design is appliquéd and then the buttons are sewn along the edges.

BEAR MOTHER is a popular

story in the Northwest Coast and Plateau areas. A woman is abducted by a BEAR and has his children. She ultimately betrays the bear to her brothers, who kill him, and she returns home.

In a HAIDA version, accounting for the origins of the Raven CLAN crest, two young lovers were prevented from marrying because they both belonged to the Raven clan. They ran away to the woods, but a bear abducted the girl, and the boy fled. He lost hope of finding her, and so she remained with the bear and had his children. After years of desperation, however, the young man returned to the forest, rescued his lover and they were allowed to remain together. The KOOTENAY variation on this version again ends with betrayal and the bear's death at the hands of the girl's brothers.

BEAR RITUALS are important

to the CREE, who prepare carefully for a BEAR hunt because the bear spirit is so powerful. Every aspect of the process, from the way the hunter dresses to the dividing and eating of the meat, is marked by detailed ritual prescriptions, prayers and offerings. The feast takes place in a feast lodge, accompanied by much ritual and enjoyment. The hunter, always mindful of the need to respect the bear spirit, cuts a piece of meat from the bear's heart and throws it in the fire, praying to Memekwesiw to grant more bears. At the end of the feast, the LODGE is opened, and the spirit of the bear escapes into the forest and returns to its master. If the people have followed the rituals correctly, the bear will revert to its animal form, so that the hunters may kill it again.

The story of a young Cree hero who saves his band from starvation supports this belief. A powerful hunter called Nenimis had captured all the animal spirits and locked them away in a box in his lodge, causing great suffering throughout the land. The young Cree volunteered to find the animals and free them. After travelling far, he came upon Nenimis's lodge. Nenimis told the youth he would offer him food, but unless he ate everything offered, he would die. It was a difficult test (and one looked upon with relish when times were hard), for Nenimis gave him one of every kind of animal, cooked whole, but the youth ate them all. Defeated, Nenimis abandoned the lodge and disappeared. The young hero then broke open the box, released the spirits and cut a hole in the lodge so that they could return once again to the forest.

The Cree are particularly careful to respect the skull and bones of the bear (as they are with the bones of all the animals they kill). Sometimes the successful hunter will keep the skull in his lodge overnight, to induce DREAMS of bears that will give him luck in the future, but then the group dispose of the remains in ritual fashion. They do not allow dogs near them, because dogs are unclean, so they hang the bones from a specially prepared tree. They strip the tree of most of its bark and branches, leaving only a small tuft of new growth at the top, and they paint it from the bottom up in ochre or vermilion, with horizontal red stripes. Then they paint circle and bar designs in vermilion on the bear's skull, stick tobacco in the jaw, tie ribbons of hide and cloth to it, and lash it to the tree.

DANCE is used to celebrate the practical and spiritual significance of the bear by many tribal peoples. As they move to the sound of drums, the dancers assume the spirit of the bear, giving them the power and wisdom necessary for successful hunting.

THE BEAVER [Dunne-za] tribe is an Athapascan-speaking hunting and gathering people who live in the forests and parklands of the Peace River region of north-western Alberta and adjoining British Columbia. They traditionally hunt moose, deer, buffalo and small game, and gather roots, berries and other wild plants. At least half the 600 members of the tribe continue to speak the native language.

BEAVER WIFE (*OJIBWAY*) is a story that teaches respect for animals. A long time ago, a young woman was fasting to help resolve her emotional problems, when a strange man appeared to her and asked her to live with him in his home at the edge of a lake. It was a wonderful place, with everything she could want in food and clothing and shelter. She soon became pregnant and – strangely – bore four children. Life was pleasant, she wanted for nothing, and she busied herself making reed mats and bags. It was only when a man came by that she realized she had married a beaver!

Over the years she bore many young, and every spring she would send them out into the world. Often her husband and children would go with the man and return

with trade goods: kettles and bowls, knives and tobacco. It was a time when people and beavers lived in harmony – the people took beavers for their pelts, but the spirits quickly returned in an endless cycle of renewed life. When the couple grew old, the husband told the wife that she must return to her human home, as he had to return to his own spirit master.

After he was gone, she stayed in her house and continued her work until one day a man tried to break into the beaver lodge, and she cried out. The man feared she was a *MANITOU*, but when he reached down through the hole and felt her head, he knew she was neither that nor a beaver. She climbed out of the lodge, an old woman with beautiful white hair, a wonderful cloth skirt, a beaded cloak, pretty moccasins and earrings. She lived a long time among her people and taught them to respect the beaver always, so that they would never be without its wonderful pelt. (See also *SPIRITS OF THE EARTH*)

BEGOCIDI (*NAVAJO*), "One-Who-Grabs-Breasts", a *TRICKSTER* who represents the darker side of the human spirit. In some situations he has a rapacious sexual appetite, causing women who sub-

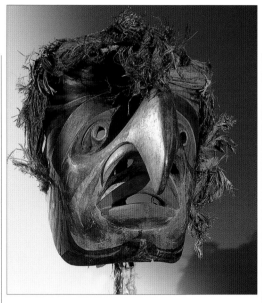

mit to his unnatural and improper advances to give birth to monsters, and in others he is a transvestite. He is also the first potter and in some versions is a creator (as he was a child of the Sun).

THE BELLA COOLA are Salishan speakers who occupy a section of the rugged coastal region of British Columbia, just to the north of Vancouver Island. This is a region with a mild climate, coastal seas teeming with sea mammals and fish, vast beds of shellfish

A BELLA COOLA MASK, collected in 1913, representing one of the ancestors of humankind. The creator employed four carpenters to carve these beings in the form of birds and animals. This ancestor flew to earth as an eagle.

along the shores, rivers with an abundance of salmon and trout, and deep forests with deer and other game and a wide variety of plants. It provided sufficient resources for hunters and gatherers to develop an affluent way of life more akin to that of agriculturalists. Their stratified society of elites, commoners and slaves was organized by family and clan. They lived in permanent villages of cedar-plank houses, and developed a complex and striking visual art, including monumental *TOTEM POLES*, intricately carved household goods and woven baskets, that evoked the ancestral animal beings believed to be responsible for their origins.

THE BEAVER creates a safe and secure home by using construction techniques that are surprisingly human. Since it spends most of its time in the water, the beaver builds a dam to flood an area of sufficient depth to build a lodge of mud and sticks with an underwater entrance.

BIBLE STORIES were a potent weapon in the hands of missionaries, as their simple narratives had themselves emerged from mythological traditions in the Middle East. Biblical teachings influenced some story-tellers to the extent that they adapted Bible stories into the context of native situations.

The *CHOCTAW*, for example, relate a version of the Tower of Babel. There was originally only one race of people, the Choctaw, fashioned by the Creator out of yellow clay (this is a different version of creation from the Choctaw emergence myth of *NANIH WAIYA*). They were content, but they were curious about what the blue sky and clouds might be, so they decided to build a tower to reach the sky. After the first day of piling rocks to build the mound, a wind came in the night and blew it down. They started again the next day, but that night the winds blew it down again. On the third night, the wind was so strong that the whole structure came crashing down upon them. Strangely, they survived, but when they came up from beneath the rocks and tried to speak to one another, they found that they spoke different languages and could no longer understand one another. The people who still spoke Choctaw remained, but the others scattered across the continent and formed all the different tribes that exist today.

BIG BLACK METEORIC STAR (*PAWNEE*) is a star northwest of the Morning Star. It controls all animals, especially the buffalo, and is responsible for the coming of the night.

BIRD NESTER is a widespread theme reflecting the psychological tensions related to family life. A father and son compete for the same woman. The father sends the son to climb to a high nest but, so that he can take the woman, he removes the ladder and maroons

the boy. Ultimately, however, the son is rescued by supernatural beings and takes revenge on the father. For a *YUROK* version of this theme, see *COYOTE*.

THE BLACKFOOT (or Blackfeet) [Blackfoot, Blood, Northern Piegan, Piegan] consist of four related Algonquian-speaking tribes occupying lands in northwestern Montana and southern Alberta: the Piegan in Montana, and the Northern Piegan, Blood and Blackfoot in Alberta. They seem to have moved westwards from Saskatchewan during the 18th century and ranged widely in the Northern Plains, following the great buffalo herds, which provided them with food, clothing and other essential resources. They were traditional allies of the *SARCEE* and the *GROS VENTRE* in the Blackfoot Confederacy. (See also *TRANSFORMATION, SPIRITS OF THE EARTH*)

BLESSINGWAY (*NAVAJO*) is a collection of stories and rituals re-enacting the creation of the present world after the emergence of people from the underworld. It includes the birth of *CHANGING WOMAN* and the founding of the Kinaalda (girls' puberty ceremony). Involved with childbirth rites, weddings and house-blessings, it is intended to secure a good, healthy life.

BLOOD CLOT (*BLACKFOOT*) is the *CULTURE HERO* Kutoyis, the

PLAINS TRIBES used a simple but effective method to transport goods and people unable to ride. The travois consists of heavy poles hauled by horses. This hand-coloured photograph shows a Blackfoot family in the foothills of the Rocky Mountains c. 1900.

adopted son of First Man and First Woman. He was the miscarried foetus of a buffalo cow (hence his name, which refers to the placenta). In heroic fashion, he slew giant animals and monsters – *BEARS* and rattlesnakes, for example, and Wind-sucker (a tornado), who ate people passing by – and successfully outwitted evil women.

His last mission was to destroy a monster, Blood-sucker, on the shore of a large lake. He fought with it in the water until Thunder killed it with lightning and threw it on the prairie. When his work was done, Blood Clot died and took his place, like all the dead, as one of the stars. The lake is no longer to be found, but on its dry bed lie Blood Clot's bones, and the blood-red rocks that record the battle.

BLUE JAY (*CHINOOK*) is an important *TRICKSTER* in Northwest Coast tradition. To the Coast *SALISH* he is a mere clown, but in the interior, the Salish and Penutian people of the forests regarded him more highly. The Chinook honoured him with a Blue Jay dance. *SHAMANS* would dance until overwhelmed by Blue Jay's power, at which point they would run

madly around the village, imitating the raucous call of the bird until they were brought back to the medicine lodge by their fellow tribesmen. After regaining their senses, they had gained the power to perform cures and grant wishes.

BRIGHT EYES (*PAWNEE*) was a spurned suitor in a moral tale who, after his rejection, went off and married a prairie dog (and became one). The couple eventually returned to the village, became human and led a good life, until the man once again met the woman who had rejected him. She apologized, and, in a moment of weakness, they had intercourse. Because of this transgression, the man's wife and children returned to the prairie dog town, and he died of a broken heart.

THE PRAIRIE DOG (Cynomys ludovicianus) is a small, hamster-like rodent of the plains and plateaux of the west. It is a social animal that lives in a network of burrows and tunnels in warrens, called "towns", with distinct social units called coteries. When an intruder enters the area, the prairie dog gives out a sharp barking alarm that quickly alerts the colony. In 1901, one extended town in the plains covered an area of 160 x 386 km (100 x 240 miles) and contained 400,000,000 prairie dogs. They have been exterminated in most of their territory by ranchers.

TRANSFORMATION

A HUMAN LIFE IS SO BRIEF that the face of the earth seems absolute and unchanging. No living being has seen the billions of years of tectonic shifts, overwhelming seas and ice ages that have scarred the land, so the idea of a decaying world is almost unimaginable. Someone with superhuman power must have made the rivers, as we might trace a line in the sand. And someone must have given us the gifts of nature that we use to sustain our lives. In aboriginal thought, the time when powerful beings transformed creation's dark, empty lands into the familiar, sheltering earth is only just out of reach of memory. Life at that time was fluid. Those first ancestors shifted and changed form at will between humans,

animals and objects as they carried out their formative tasks – bringing daylight and fire, hewing out the shape of the land and creating the stuff of cultural life. Raven, Coyote and the other transformers are not the props of a simple animal worship, but emerged from the elders' awareness that the supernaturals had withdrawn from the world they created – just as the knowing raven and the sly coyote circle on the edges of human culture today.

A SHAMAN (right) needed contact with the spiritual forces of nature to ensure the health and wellbeing of a tribal society. To attract, entice or control these forces, shamans sought out worldly objects with special qualities that gave them great medicine power. Here, a Blackfoot shaman, dressed to cure illness, wears the pelt of a bear and is festooned with the skins of snakes, and other talismans of the animal beings at the core of life. (19TH-CENTURY PAINTING BY GEORGE CATLIN.)

SHAMANS (below) moved among the beings of the spirit world, so people feared and respected them. In a modern pencil drawing by a Baker Lake Inuit artist, the spirit of a dead shaman comes back to provide food for her descendants. Inuit people believe that the spirits of shamans remain in the land, so they avoid their gathering places. The people of Baker Lake talk of two small islands where these restless spirits seem to dwell, as hunters who have camped there have lost valuable equipment, supplies and dogs. (DRAWING BY RUTH ANNAQTUUSI TULURIALIK, 1985.)

A FAMILIAR LANDSCAPE (above) transformed from a featureless world is a great story that is preserved in the contours and features of the earth. Raven created the Queen Charlotte Islands, the land of the Haida, because he was tired of flying and had no place to rest on the primordial waters. He created the land by dropping stones in the water or, in another version, by splashing the water and turning the spray into rock.

TRANSFORMATION (right) was not only a spiritual concept, but also a practical necessity, especially before the introduction of the swift-footed horse. In prehistoric times, hunters had to stalk game on foot, so they often adopted the guise of animals in order to move close enough to shoot them with their arrows. In this woodcut, two hunters draped – perhaps surprisingly – in wolf skins crawl towards a herd of buffalo. (EDUARD VERMORCKEN, AFTER A PAINTING BY GEORGE CATLIN, 1848.)

C

BRIGHT-CLOUD WOMAN (*TSIMSHIAN*) is the provider and protector of salmon. She married the trickster *RAVEN*, with predictable consequences: Raven got greedy, gambled away his salmon stocks, and she abandoned him.

BROTHER GODS (*MOJAVE*) were creator-*TRANSFORMERS* who formed (along with all other creatures) when earth and sky touched. One, Matavilya, led the people to the centre of the world, built the first house and, after unintentionally making sexual overtures to his daughter, sickened, died and became the first cremation (during which *COYOTE* stole his heart). The other, Mastamho, after making the Colorado River and causing a flood, led the people to a sacred mountain (Avikwame) where he taught them Mojave culture and imbued their *SHAMANS* with dream power.

THE COLORADO RIVER was created by one of the Brother Gods. Its turquoise-green ribbon is a miraculous sight in the deserts of Arizona, providing life-giving water and a mirror that joins the earth and sky.

THE BUFFALO CAP (*CHEYENNE*) is a very sacred object associated with the *SUN DANCE* origin myth. Seeking to end a terrible famine, a young *SHAMAN* (eventually to be named Erect Horns), entered an opening in the middle of a mountain and encountered Great Medicine. This spirit taught him the

Sun Dance and gave him the buffalo cap to wear during the ritual. When he returned to his people and instructed them in the ceremony, they were able to overcome the famine and ensure a plentiful supply of buffalo in the future.

BUFFALO HUSBAND (*BLACK-FOOT*) is a story that relates the origins of the Ikunuhkahtsi (Bull Dance). A bull buffalo took a woman as a wife. When her father tried to rescue her, the buffalo killed him. However, the woman brought her father back to life, so the bull husband taught him the Bull Dance ceremony (intended to propitiate the buffalo spirit), and the father and daughter were allowed to return to their home.

BUFFALO WIFE figures in a widespread Plains myth which accounts for the origin of the buffalo-hunting tradition. The people hunted buffalo with little success until a man married a buffalo woman. She took him to her

THE GRAND TETONS rise abruptly into the skies above the lush grasslands of the Snake River valley in Wyoming. For the native peoples who hunted buffalo on the plains, these great landmarks were important parts of their sacred lands.

homeland and taught him how to use a bow to kill the animal, as well as how to prepare the meat. He brought the knowledge back to his people, and forever afterwards they hunted and caught buffalo with great ease.

BUFFALO WOMAN (*CHEYENNE, PAWNEE*) is involved in a Great Race theme, in which animals and birds once raced between Mato Tipila (*DEVIL'S TOWER*) and the Teton Mountains (both in Wyoming) in order to prove which was the greatest. In an arrogant move, a buffalo woman was chosen to represent her species, but Hawk (prairie falcon) defeated her, ensuring that humans and birds would always rule over other animals.

THE BUFFALO was hunted before the introduction of the horse, when hunters had to outwit it to capture it. They would ambush the animals as they grazed in gullies or arroyos, or travelled along narrow valley edges, and in some places they stampeded the animals over steep cliffs.

BUKWUS (*KWAKIUTL*) is a monstrous spirit who dwells in the dark rainforests of the Pacific coast. Although he is repulsive, he has a fierce longing for companionship. With his beautiful singing voice, he attracts to his home the spirits of those who have drowned.

CARIBOU MOTHER (Central and Eastern *INUIT*) is the mistress of the caribou. In an Igulik account, there were no caribou

A MODERN BUKWUS MASK records the strong, fierce qualities of this wild monster of the forests.

until an old woman went inland and fashioned them from her breeches. The original caribou was dangerous, as it had sharp fangs and tusks. After one of these monsters killed a hunter, the old woman went back inland, gathered them all together, knocked out the sharp front teeth and changed the tusks into antlers. Then she gave them each a kick on the forehead, creating the hollow that can still be seen to this day, and they ran off. Unfortunately, hunters still had difficulty killing the caribou, because the hair on the woman's breeches all lay in one direction, and the streamlined caribou ran like the wind. So she gathered them together again and made the hair lie in different patterns, slowing them down enough to be hunted. Her work done, the old woman went to live with the caribou and never returned to the human world.

CAYUGA see *IROQUOIS*.

THE CELESTIAL CANOE

(*ALABAMA*) relates to the movement of stars through the seasons and the effects these movements have on the natural world. The Alabama refer to the bowl of the Big Dipper (the Plough) as the Boat Stars. To their *CREEK* neighbours, it is a distinct constellation: Pilohabi, meaning "image of a canoe". It is a potent seasonal marker, as it first

falls to the horizon and rises again in late July. This is the time of the Green Corn (Maize) Ceremony celebrated by these southeastern peoples, when the first corn ripens. Among the Alabama, the supporting myth contains elements also found in the Green Corn Ceremony, including dancing, feasting and a *STICK-AND-BALL GAME*.

Visitors from the sky descended to the earth in a canoe to play stick-ball on a prairie, then ascended again into the sky. A man witnessed this daily occurrence, and one day captured one of the women and took her as his wife. She bore children and had a pleasant life, but she yearned for her home in the sky, so she went out to the prairie with her children and climbed into the boat as it rested there. However, the attempt failed, because her husband returned from hunting unexpectedly and pulled them back to earth. Then the mother secretly built a second, smaller, canoe for her children, and she tried again. This time she succeeded, rising into the night sky in the big canoe, but her husband managed to grab and hold back the smaller canoe with the children in it. Eventually the father agreed to take the now-grieving children into the sky to find their mother. An old woman in her sky *LODGE* fed the children squash and corn cobs, and then directed them to another house where they found their mother dancing. Once again they all returned to earth, but after a time the still-unhappy woman finally took her children in the big canoe and left the earth forever. The husband tried to follow in the smaller canoe, but when he looked down he fell to earth and was killed.

THE GREAT BEAR, Big Dipper or Plough is one of the most striking constellations in the northern sky. Because the arrangement of stars is so clear, and it rises and sets in a predictable cycle through the year, it was an important marker of seasonal change among many northern peoples.

CHANGING WOMAN (Estsánatlehi) (*NAVAJO*) was so named

because she has the power to grow old and become young again, following the rhythm of the earth's seasons. First Man ('Áltsé Hastiin) and First Woman ('Áltsé 'Asdzáá), two of the beings from the First, or Black, World (*SPIDER WOMAN* was another), discovered her in a raincloud on top of a mountain. They fed her on pollen and dew, and she grew rapidly. After puberty, she exposed her body to sun and water and conceived the *TWIN* war gods, *NAYENEZGANI AND TOBADJISH-TCHINI*. After her sons had made the world safe from monsters, she went to live on an island beyond the western sea. By dancing on the four directions, she produced rain clouds (east), fabrics and jewels (south), plant life (west) and corn (maize) and animals (north). She figures prominently in the Navajo ritual complex called *BLESSINGWAY*. For an *APACHE* version of this myth, see *WHITE-PAINTED WOMAN*.

THE CHEHALIS [Lower, Upper] are two small tribes who

once occupied a territory that stretched along the Chehalis River in present-day southwest Washington State. They speak closely related Salishan languages.

The Upper Chehalis lived among the headwaters of the river, and so pursued a traditional

interior hunting and gathering life, whereas the Lower Chehalis lived at the river's mouth, where they could also exploit the resources of the sea. They now occupy the Colville Reservation in northeast Washington State, along with the remnants of a number of small regional tribes.

CHÉMSEN see *RAVEN*.

THE CHEROKEE, an Iroquoian-speaking people, once

controlled a vast territory that spread across the southeastern United States. It included the Carolinas, the Virginias, Kentucky, Tennessee, Georgia and Alabama. They grew corn (maize) and other crops in the fertile river valleys, and hunted and gathered according to the seasons.

After various treaties in the 18th and early 19th centuries restricted them to infertile mountainous areas, the US government forced them to leave their ancestral lands in 1838 and 1839 to journey over 1,600 km (1,000 miles) to Indian Territory (in present-day Oklahoma). Many Cherokee perished, while others refused to leave, and took refuge in the mountains. Although the majority of Cherokee now live in northeastern Oklahoma, they still retain a small but vital presence in North Carolina. (See also *NEW GODS*)

THE CHEYENNE [Northern, Southern] people are an Algonquian-speaking tribe that probably originated in the prairies and mixed woodlands of the upper Mississippi Valley region and gradually spread into the northeastern Great Plains. After the horse was introduced to the region in the 18th century, they took up the traditional Plains buffalo-hunting life, following the herds and using the animals for food, clothing and other material necessities. Their territory at this time was so vast, stretching from the Yellowstone River in Montana to the upper Arkansas River in Colorado and Kansas, that they became separated into northern and southern groups.

The Northern Cheyenne now live on the Tongue River Reservation in Montana, and the Southern Cheyenne occupy land allotments in Oklahoma.

CHIBIABOS (FOX, POTAWATOMI) was the wolf brother of the culture hero WISAKEDJAK (or NANABUSH). He was the ruler of the dead.

DULL KNIFE (1810–1883), a Northern Cheyenne chief, tried to lead his people 2,400 km (1,500 miles) back to their ancestral homeland in Montana after being forcibly removed to Oklahoma. When their struggle roused public sentiment, the government granted them a reservation.

CHILD-OF-THE-WATER (Chiricahua APACHE) is a CULTURE HERO who was born after WHITE-PAINTED WOMAN conceived a child by letting the rain fall on her navel or vagina (note the similarity here to the NAVAJO stories of CHANGING WOMAN and NAYENEZGANI AND TOBADJISHTCHINI). The boy slew the monsters responsible for killing human beings – a giant (see LAND-SCAPE), an antelope that killed with its eyes, monster eagles and a buffalo. Two narrative fragments give different versions of the creation of human beings. In one, Child-of-the-Water created them out of mud figures; in the other, he enveloped himself in a dark cloud and disappeared, leaving in his place the first two human beings.

THE CHINOOK were members of a large Penutian-speaking tribe that once occupied coastal lands in Washington State and the Lower Columbia River basin in Oregon and Washington. They fished, hunted and gathered the marine life along the Pacific coast and journeyed up the inland rivers to take salmon and trout. Their language developed a pidgin form, Chinook Wawa, which became a trading language along the coast from Oregon to Alaska. Disease and dislocation drastically reduced their numbers after white settlement. They now live on allotments at Quinault, on Washington's Olympic Peninsula.

THE CHIPEWYAN live in the vast northern forests to the west of Hudson Bay, from the Churchill River in Manitoba to Lake Athabasca in northern Saskatchewan and Alberta to Great Slave Lake in the Northwest Territories. They are the largest of the DENE, a group of closely related Athapascan peoples, which also include the Slavey (or Slave), the Dogrib, Yellowknife and Sahtu. These semi-nomadic groups travelled in small bands in a seasonal round along the innumerable rivers and lakes of the boreal forests

A CHOCTAW HOUSE fashioned from palmetto leaves attached to a pole frame. The loose construction allowed air to circulate in the hot and humid climate.

and the edge of the treeless Arctic barrens, hunting caribou, moose, deer, bear and other game animals, catching waterfowl and gathering berries and other plant foods. While the fur trade established a dependency on a Western economic system, their remoteness from centres of modern culture has enabled them to retain many of their traditional practices and beliefs.

CHIPPEWA see under OJIBWAY.

THE CHOCTAW people are a Muskogean-speaking tribe that lived in the area of present-day Mississippi. The river valleys provided an abundance of plant and animal life, deer, waterfowl, turkeys, nuts and grasses, and the fertile soil supported corn (maize), beans and other crops. The agricultural base of these and other Mississippian peoples supported a well-organized society. It has many of the religious features associated with Mesoamerican influences, such as sun worship, raised earthen ceremonial plazas, burial mounds, and common iconographic elements in art and religion.

Between 1830 and 1836, the government removed most of the tribe to Indian Territory (in present-day Oklahoma), causing great loss of life. Today, the Mississippi Choctaws live in small rural settlements scattered across the state, whereas the Oklahoma Choctaws are centred in Tuskahoma.

CHRISTIAN TEACHINGS have worked their way into the structure and content of ancient oral traditions. Although beliefs about singular creators, primeval waters and great floods may predate the Biblical epics, it is impossible to differentiate these very ancient resonances from the intense ideological impact of more than 500 years of missionary activity in North America.

One unfortunate consequence of this religious proselytizing was the demotion of traditional CULTURE HEROES in favour of the Christian repertoire. This is strikingly clear in a modern narrative of the BEAVER tribe's culture hero Saya. He transformed the animal people into the animals we see today, and he was the first hunter. When Saya travelled to the land of the dead, he followed a long path around the rim of the world (like YAMANHDEYA, the culture hero of the Beaver's northerly neighbours, the *DENE*) but now, as the story explains, this travail is no longer necessary. *JESUS* has made a straight cut (short cut) directly to heaven.

THE CHUMASH people are

a small tribe that once occupied the offshore islands and coasts of southern California in the area of present-day Santa Barbara, where they prospered on the abundant deep-sea and coastal food resources of the Pacific Ocean. Spanish influence almost overwhelmed their rich culture, and the last known speaker of any of the five Chumash languages (of the Hokan family) died in 1965. Work by an anthropologist in the first half of the 20th century, however, provided enough ethnographic evidence to help support a Chumash cultural revival that has taken place in the past 20 years.

CLANS, like all tribal institutions,

have origins within the belief systems of their people. A clan is a group of related families in a tribal culture that traces its origins to a specific mythological ancestor. Clan origins are therefore an important part of narratives about events that took place when the world was taking shape.

When the *HOPI* people began emerging from the First World, for example, they started to hunt for

A MORALISTIC TABLEAU, set at the Spanish Mission of the Alamo in Texas, shows a group of Spanish men gambling outside the mission. They contrast starkly with the devout Indian people kneeling in the background.

the rising sun. The first band came upon a dead *BEAR*, so it became the Bear Clan, the second came upon the same skeleton but found gopher holes around it and became the Gopher Clan. Other Hopis, who travelled much more slowly, as they had many children, found a nest of spiders and named themselves the Spider Clan. This particular clan made a fortuitous choice, for they gained the protection of the wise and powerful grandmother, *SPIDER WOMAN*. To help them in their journey, she took dust from their bodies and fashioned the first burro to carry their heaviest loads. The Bear Clan, which arrived first and quickly established its village, remains a powerful group. Although the Spider Clan was the last to arrive, it became the biggest Hopi clan because of the large number of children its ancestors brought with them on their journey.

THE COCHITI, a Keresan-

speaking *PUEBLO* culture, live along the Rio Grande in north central New Mexico. In order to farm in

this dry region, they practise irrigation. They retain their traditional social structures, including two moieties (an anthropological classification for the two halves into which all the *CLANS* are divided), the Turquoise Kiva and the Pumpkin Kiva, about a dozen clans, and numerous *SECRET SOCIETIES*, but they are mainly practising Catholics.

THE COLVILLE people are a

small Salishan tribe living in the rugged Plateau region of northeastern Washington State. Before the coming of the *WHITE MAN*, they fished the local rivers for salmon, and supplemented their diet with deer and other small game and plant foods. They were uprooted during the 19th century, when a motley collection of prospectors, miners, loggers and settlers invaded their territory, and they are now consolidated in an extremely complex organization of at least 16 tribes in the Colville Reservation.

THE COMANCHE (Nemene)

were once a nomadic hunting and gathering people, speaking an Uto-

PUEBLO tribes strongly resisted the incursions of Spanish and American peoples, even as Catholic missionaries spread Christianity among them. Pecos Mission church, at Pecos Pueblo, New Mexico, was the seat of the Pueblo Revolt of 1688, when the tribe rose up against the Spanish.

Aztecan language, who ranged from the Rocky Mountains into the interior of Mexico. In 1867, the US government compelled them to sign the Medicine Lodge Treaty, which removed them to a reservation in southwest Oklahoma, but in 1887 the General Allotment Act dissolved the reservation, allotted 65 ha (160 acres) of land to each adult, reserved a small amount of land for future tribal members, and distributed the remaining thousands of acres to non-Indian settlers. In spite of their lack of territory, the Comanche retain many aspects of their traditional culture and are especially noted for their elaborate dance costumes, which contain fine feather and beadwork.

COPPER WOMAN (CHIPE-

WYAN, DENE) figures in a story related to the origins of native copper, found in the north on the Copper and Coppermine Rivers.

Once an *INUIT* abducted a woman, but she escaped and, while fleeing home, discovered yellow nuggets. She guided a hunting party back to the spot to see these strange stones, but the men could not resist molesting her. Her honour violated, she sank into the ground in shame, and the men left offerings of meat to make up for their transgressions. Now known as Copper Woman, she transformed these offerings into copper.

THE LIVING SKY

T HE SKY MUST BE THE REALM OF GODS. Well beyond the reach of even the highest mountains, the greatest powers reside there – light and darkness, the changing seasons, furious storms and life-giving rains – and it is the source of many creations.

Some remote creators used the dark cosmos as a staging ground for their work, but in most narratives the sky was a world with its own physical and social dimensions, not an airless void. In an Iroquois version, for example, a young woman fell through a hole in the sky world, and the birds and water animals had to create dry earth to support her. The heavens may also be a final resting place for supernatural beings who are transformed into stars. The sky is crucial to cultural identity, because it defines the land and sets the rhythm of the world. The cycles of the sun, moon and stars evoke a sense of time, marking the passage of human lives. As a measure of space and time, the sky therefore unites the mythical and the actual in an eternal flow of darkness and light.

THE MOON MASK (above) of a Tlingit shaman reflects the common perception of the moon as a being with human attributes. For the Tlingit and other Northwest Coast tribes, the significance of the moon was not simply in its cosmological origins, but in its control of the rising and falling of the tides crucial to life on the edge of the Pacific Ocean. The mask, carved in cedar c. 1840–70, enabled the shaman to draw some of the power of this great sky being.

THE FURY OF STORMS (above) shows the overwhelming power of the beings in the sky world. The idea of thunder and lightning as the work of a giant thunderbird makes sense in an animate universe. The dark storm line, edged with lightning, rampages over the land and is gone, just like a hawk or eagle in flight, hunting for food.

THE PLEIADES (above), known to astronomers as Messier 45, is an open star cluster (top right) approximately 410 light years from earth . It plays an important role in many tribal mythologies, often as seven maidens, one of which (the dimmest star) is veiled or has fallen to earth. For the Pawnee, these stars symbolize unity.

THE GRANITE CEILING (above) of an Algonquian shaman's cave near the Lake of the Woods in northwestern Ontario is painted with red ochre images of stars and forms that may represent celestial beings. In prehistoric times, the night sky was crucial as a knowledge resource – a device for thinking about history and the world of the spirit.

CORN MAIDENS

CORN MAIDENS (*ZUNI*) are personifications of corn (maize), whose role in Zuni agriculture is re-enacted in the Corn Dance.

In one version of the narrative, Corn Maidens accompanied the first people to the surface of the earth, but they were invisible until two witches, the last people to emerge, perceived them. Recognizing their power, the witches gave them corn and squash seeds. The first people continued their journey, leaving the maidens at Shipololo (place of mist and cloud) where they lived in a cedar bower roofed with clouds. There they danced. When the Ahayuta (warrior *TWINS*) discovered the maidens, they brought them back to the people, whom starvation always threatened. The maidens danced in a courtyard decorated with cornmeal paintings of clouds. After the butterfly and flower god Payatami lusted after Yellow-Corn Maiden, however, the maidens fled back to Shipololo. A terrible famine ensued, until at last the Ahayuta brought them back to the settle-ment. The Corn Dance ensures that these important gods are properly respected, so that they will always remain among the Zuni.

CORN MOTHER

CORN MOTHER, as the mistress of corn (maize), is associated with all aspects of the cultivation of this important crop.

To the Keresan and Isleta *PUEBLO*, she is one of two sister deities born in the underworld. In one version of the myth, before the emergence of human beings into the present world, Thought Woman gave the two sisters baskets of seeds and images representing all future beings; in another, Corn Mother planted bits of her heart in the ground, and the corn sprouted up. In the *IROQUOIS* version, the corn stalks spring from Corn Mother's breasts. Western *ABENAKI* people say that corn tassels are yellow because the Corn Mother has yellow hair.

A *CHEROKEE* story explains why corn requires special cultivation and matures slowly over a single season each year. The Cherokee corn mother is Selu, the wife of the *MASTER OF ANIMALS*, Kanáti. After her two sons, Good Boy and He-Who-Grew-Up-Wild, released all their father's game animals, and the family had nothing but corn and beans to eat, the boys noticed that their mother's storehouse had an endless supply. One day they followed her and discovered that she produced corn by rubbing her abdomen, and beans by rubbing her legs (or, in another version, armpits). Fearing that she was a witch (or offended by the source of the food), the boys refused to eat. With her secret out, Selu told her sons that she would soon die. To cushion their loss, she instructed them to clear a patch of ground, drag her clothes over the surface and watch by night; in the morning they would find a field of corn. Unfortunately, when she died, the boys cleared only seven small patches. Consequently, corn does not grow everywhere. And, because they tired of the nightly vigil, the corn stopped maturing quickly, and now takes an entire summer season to grow.

COTSIPAMAPOT

COTSIPAMAPOT (Moapa), the old woman creator, scattered earth around her island, making all the creatures of the world – including one man. Her daughter could not mate with this man because she had a toothed vagina, but Cotsi-pamapot told him how to grind down the teeth. The couple eventually had children – the first people – and the old woman had them placed in the centre of the Moapa world.

COTTONTAIL

COTTONTAIL (Great Basin) is a *TRICKSTER* who lacks any of the redeeming features of the *CULTURE HEROES*, causing havoc even for that inveterate trickster *COYOTE*. Cottontail once made war on the sun, either to reduce its excessive warmth or put it higher in the sky, regardless of its effects on the people. His rather brutal nature is made clear in a northern *PAIUTE* version of the story, in which he went to the home of the North Wind, seduced its daughter and burned her alive with all her brothers.

A COUNCIL OF ANIMALS

A COUNCIL OF ANIMALS constitutes the common decision-making process in mythologies. When there is a problem to resolve, the supernatural animal people hold a council, just as humans do. This reflects the common native belief that animals have societies resembling human ones, with similar forms of social organization. This democratic approach contrasts with the Christian idea of a single omnipotent creator.

The most widespread example of an animal council at work is in the *EARTH DIVER* creation story. For the *TUSKEGEE*, the entire creation was the result of a debate. Some of the birds – the only creatures who

quarrel, and eventually moved to a second world, where they discovered bigger insects and monstrous animals. When they escaped into a third world, Coyote inexplicably kidnapped a water monster's baby, causing a great flood. To save the people, First Man planted a reed that rose into the sky; the people climbed it and emerged into the present world.

In California, the coastal MIWOK say that Coyote created the earth by shaking his blanket over the primeval waters, causing them to dry up, while the MAIDU rank him with EARTH-MAKER as one of the two original beings. To the Maidu, Earth-maker represented an abstract potential for creation. Coyote carried it out, and caused DEATH in the real world. Coyote is responsible for human death in a CHINOOK story with an Orpheus-like theme, in which he and EAGLE travelled to the land of the dead to retrieve their wives. They came upon an enormous lodge, where they discovered that the dead only appear when an old woman creates darkness by swallowing the moon. To rescue their wives, Coyote killed the woman, swallowed the moon and gathered up all the dead in a box. When the two heroes started back, Coyote was so anxious to see his wife, whose voice he heard, that he lifted the lid, and all the dead

rose up in a cloud and disappeared. If he had been patient and waited until they had returned home to open the box, there would be no death in the world today.

For all his weaknesses, Coyote is the consummate transformer. In the Great Basin, he created earth by pouring sand on the primeval waters, created light, stole fire, stole pine nuts and released impounded game animals. The WAPPO of California credit him with the origin of language, as he stole the bag of words from Old Man MOON. In the Plateau region, the SANPOIL believe he releases the salmon.

In a YUROK myth, he is even responsible for the money supply (the Yurok, like many coastal peoples, having a strong sense of property and its value in exchange). In this scenario, Coyote was a sinful father who stranded his son in a nest high up a tree so that he could seduce the young man's two wives (a version of the universal BIRD NESTER theme). When the son finally climbed down, he was so angry that he stole all the wealth of the tribe (DENTALIUM SHELLS), but Coyote managed to get it back, and redistributed it.

THE COYOTE lives and hunts close to areas of human settlement, but it is seldom seen except by its tracks, like these in the desert sands of Nevada.

could live in a world of air and water – wanted land, in order to increase their food supply, but others wanted things to remain the same. To resolve the issue, they appointed EAGLE as chief, and asked him to decide. He supported the argument in favour of land, and asked for a volunteer to search for some. Dove accepted the challenge, but he flew across the skies and saw nothing but endless water. Then Crawfish dived deep into the water and returned with a bit of mud in his claws. Eagle took this mud and made an island. As the waters began to fall, the island got bigger and bigger, until other islands emerged to join into a single earth.

COYOTE

COYOTE is a complex and fascinating CULTURE HERO, varying from tribe to tribe between wise TRANSFORMER and bumbling TRICKSTER. Agriculturalists tend to regard him as a crude and dispensable pest.

In a typical HOPI story, for example, Coyote was a sheep-stealer who harassed their flocks until they drove him into NAVAJO lands, where

THE ANIMAL GUARDIANS of tribal peoples keep council about the trials of life as do their human relatives. In this work by an Onondaga artist, the animal ancestors of Iroquois clans gather by the Tree of Peace, the symbol of unity of the Iroquois peoples. (PAINTING BY ARNOLD JACOBS.)

a Navajo shepherd outwitted him and burned him alive in a SWEAT-LODGE. The Hopi use the epithet "ihu", which means both coyote and sucker, for a person easily fooled.

To hunters and gatherers, however, Coyote is a resourceful creature, with a strong will to survive – but, just like humans, he is sometimes the victim of his own devious ways. This contradictory status is evident in a Navajo CREATION story, re-enacted during a nine-day ceremony, in which one of his pranks ended up causing the emergence of the Navajo into the present world. He lived in Black World, an island-like place floating in mist. Only ants and other insect-people inhabited it until the touching of two clouds created First Man and First Woman. As the population grew, the group began to

CREATION accounts attribute the origin of the earth and sky, humans and other living things to the actions of supernatural beings. While accounts of a singular creator, a Great Spirit, are now relatively common across the continent, this fundamentally hierarchical religious structure is most consistent with the structured agricultural societies of the Southwest. The *ZUNI* creator, for example, is the sun (Yatokka taccu, the Sun Father), the most powerful object in the sky.

The drama of creation, unique for each tribal group, resolves into several general scenarios. In the *EARTH DIVER* theme, the emphasis is not on the origin of the cosmos, but on the practical need to create some land on which to live. In a *CHEROKEE* version, the original world, made of solid rock, sat above the sky, but its inhabitants had a problem: it was getting overcrowded, and there was nothing but water below. After much discussion, the water beetle, called Beaver's Grandchild, agreed to go down, and eventually came back with some soft mud, which began to grow and formed the earth. For an *ARAPAHO* version, see *FLAT PIPE*.

Another approach has supernatural beings constructing the world and its features through actions analogous to those in the human world. In an *INUIT* story from Kodiak Island, when *RAVEN* got light from the sky, a bladder descended containing a man and a woman. As they struggled, they stretched the bladder until it formed the world, with hills and mountains rising up where they pushed at the walls with their hands and feet. The man's hair became the forest and all its animals, the woman made seas by urinating, and rivers and lakes by spitting into ditches and holes, and when the man used one of the woman's teeth as a knife to carve wood, the woodchips became fish. The most crucial transformation of all took place when one of the

couple's sons played with a stone that became an island. The *TRANSFORMER* put another son and a female dog on the island and set it afloat. When it came to rest, it was Kodiak Island, and the boy and his dog wife became the ancestors of all the Kodiak Island people.

The concepts of impregnation, gestation and birth also figure in a variety of accounts. In one Great Basin narrative, a young woman and her mother lived on a small island, perhaps the only people in the world. It was a lonely life, so the mother sent the daughter out to find a mate, and she eventually came back with *COYOTE*. As there is no life without struggle, Coyote first had to overcome one serious obstacle. His new wife had a toothed vagina. Fortunately, he was able to jam it with a stick of wood and impregnate her. She gave birth to many tiny babies, and as she did, she dropped them into a wicker pitcher. When the pitcher was full, Coyote scattered them over the land.

The emergence theme, typical of the Southwest, has within it an ancient resonance of the original hunting and gathering life. The process of creation is a long and arduous journey through a series of underworlds wracked by turmoil

and danger. The first beings in *HOPI* creation lived in the deepest of three cavernous worlds beneath the present surface. This first world was dark, crowded and filthy. As the suffering was so great, two brothers (*TWIN* warrior gods) pierced the roof of the cave and planted a cane below; it grew through the opening into a second underworld, and the people climbed up on its ladder-like joints. This second cave was also dark, and after a time it too became crowded and filthy. When the people became distressed and began to fight amongst themselves, the Twins planted another cane and they climbed into the third (highest) cave. There they had a measure of peace, for they found fire and, by the light of torches, were able to build shelters (*KIVAS*) and travel from place to place. But this world soon turned contrary. Women neglected their families so that they could dance and, in the ensuing chaos, wives mixed with wives so the husbands could not tell one from another – promiscuity reigned. Fathers even had to care for the abandoned children. To rid the world of this evil, the people finally climbed into the fourth world, the present one, in the Grand Canyon, Arizona. After much wandering, they eventually

THE CREE, when they are on their hunting grounds, make use of only those modern tools and materials that help them in their daily lives. Canvas, for example, provides a strong and lightweight shelter ideal for camps, such as this one near the eastern shore of Hudson Bay.

settled in villages, now seen as ruins in isolated places high in the mountains, in caves or in the sides of deep canyons.

The rest of creation is usually in the hands of *TRANSFORMERS*, who arrive in a barren land and leave it filled with landscapes and living things when their work is done. To the *MAKAH*, for example, the new earth consisted only of sand, grass and animal people. Then the two brothers of the Sun and Moon, the Hohoeapbess (Two-Men-Who-Changed-Things), came to earth to make it ready for the Makah. They changed the creatures according to their behaviour in the mythic age. One, a thief, they changed into a seal, so that he could not steal with his shortened arms. A great fisherman became the great blue heron; another fisherman, one who could not resist stealing other's catches, they changed into the kingfisher. And two creatures with huge appetites they changed into *RAVEN* and his wife *CROW*.

THE CREE are an Algonquian-speaking nomadic hunting and gathering people who range in small bands through vast, lake-strewn forests surrounding Hudson Bay – from Quebec in the east to Saskatchewan in the west – as well as the northern margins of the Great Plains. Caribou and other game, fish and wildfowl provide most of their sustenance. The main tribal groups are the Plains Cree, Western Wood Cree and Swampy Cree in the west, and the Mistassini Cree and Tête de Boule Cree in the east. (See also *LANDSCAPES OF MEMORY*)

THE CREEK (Muskogee) were a farming people who lived in towns and villages in what are now the states of Georgia and Alabama. Their agricultural base enabled them to develop a stratified society with considerable wealth and extensive trading networks. Their religion shared influences from Mesoamerica in the construction of earthen ceremonial plazas, religious iconography, and burial mounds. During the 18th century, they formed the Creek Confederacy, which incorporated many smaller Muskogean-speaking tribes uprooted by European settlement. Later, during the 1830s, the government forcibly moved most of these tribes to Indian Territory (Oklahoma). While most Muskogee people live in Oklahoma, the descendants of Creek groups who resisted are scattered from Florida to Alabama.

CROW (DENA) is a *CULTURE HERO* and *TRICKSTER*, interchanged in narratives with *RAVEN*. The crow is a watchful, crafty scavenger, drawn to human settlement for what it can forage. It can be loud and quarrelsome but, while hunting, it soars silently or scans the world from a perch high in a tree. The conflation of Crow with Raven may be the result of variations in story-telling, but it is also possible

A BEADED ORNAMENT was attached by a Crow warrior to his horse's bridle. The cross design represents the four sacred directions and quarters of the world.

that the two similar birds were joined more closely in traditional mythology than they are in their modern biological classifications.

THE CROW tribe are a Siouan-speaking Plains people that migrated to the Great Plains from south of the Great Lakes and took to a buffalo-hunting way of life after the introduction of the horse in the 18th century. They followed the herds and used the animals for food, clothing and other material necessities. They are historically associated with the *HIDATSA*, village horticulturalists who lived along the Missouri River. They now occupy a reservation in south-central Montana.

DEATH is thought of as just part of the creation cycle. This heart-shaped wooden charm is used in the Naxnox dance of the Tsimshian. The owl symbolizes the soul of someone who has recently died.

CULTURE HEROES are supernatural beings who inhabited the earth throughout the mythic age. As *TRANSFORMERS*, they prepared it for the everyday needs of humans. This was a time of creative ferment, so culture heroes had characteristics of humans and animals, both idealized and observed through the experience of generations of story-tellers. This combination of the real and ideal meant that the heroes varied in their behaviour from altruism to lust, deceit and other baser human instincts. Although personalities of such great complexity are not easily classified, they are often described according to where their exploits fit in this range of human aspects. A supernatural being is heroic when involved in the tasks that define the culture to come, but a *TRICKSTER* when subject to baser human desires.

DAGWANOENYENT (Seneca) is a dangerous spirit, represented by the whirlwind. The Seneca

believe she was the daughter of the North Wind.

DAKOTA See *SIOUX*.

DEATH, as well as every living thing, has a place in *CREATION* myths. The *APACHE* view the origin of death as a deliberate act, the result of a debate between *RAVEN* and *COYOTE* as to whether humans should be immortal. To decide the matter, each threw an object in the water and proclaimed that if it sank, people would ultimately die; one threw a stick, but the other threw a stone, and that is why there is death. The Jicarilla and Lipan Apache say that Raven threw in the stone; the Chiricahua Apache blame Coyote. The *UTE* see the decision as a power struggle between two *CULTURE HEROES*, Wolf and Coyote. Wolf wanted the dead buried in anthills and revived the next day, but Coyote decreed that they would be put in the ground, their families would cut their hair in mourning, and that they would never return.

D

DEGANAWIDA (Seneca) was the mythical founder of the IRO-QUOIS Confederacy. In the Seneca version he was born to a Huron virgin, matured rapidly, then crossed Lake Ontario in a white stone canoe to reform the warring Iroquois. It is said that he planted the Great Tree of Peace that is symbolic of the League of the Iroquois. This tree has four great long white roots running outwards in the four directions to guide all the people to its shade, and it has an EAGLE at the top to warn the nations in case of outside attack.

THE DELAWARE (Lenni Lenape) [Munsi, Unami] once occupied the Atlantic coast in the Delaware River region, where they grew corn (maize) and other crops and hunted and gathered according to the season. Colonial settlement forced them out before 1700. The two original groups, speaking two related Algonquian languages, scattered westwards, stopping in Pennsylvania, Ohio, Indiana, Missouri and Kansas. Some of the Munsi people live in Wisconsin and Kansas, but most have now settled on the Six Nations of the Grand River Reserve of the IROQUOIS. The Unami live in a Federal Trust Area set aside for the Delaware in western Oklahoma.

DENA (formerly Tena) [Degexit'an, Koyukon, Tanana] is an anthropological classification for three

HIAWATHA (above), the hero of Henry Wadsworth Longfellow's narrative poem The Song of Hiawatha, was a character mainly derived from stories of the Ojibway culture hero and trickster Nanabush, as he is fancifully pictured here. The Hiawatha of the tribes of the Northeast was actually Deganawida, the Mohawk founder of the Iroquois Confederacy.

related Athapascan tribal groups with similar ways of life who live in the Yukon River drainage in Alaska: the Tanana, the Koyukon and the Degexit'an (formerly known as Ingalik). These are typical subarctic peoples, who live by travelling the innumerable waterways and lakes in the boreal forests, hunting caribou, moose, deer, BEAR, beaver and other small game, catching wildfowl and fish, and gathering roots and tubers.

THE DENE are a group of closely related Athapascan peoples – including the Slavey (or Slave), Dogrib, CHIPEWYAN, Yellowknife and Sahtu – who live in the boreal forests of northern Canada from Great Bear and Great Slave Lakes east to Hudson Bay, in the Northwest Territories and south into northern Alberta, Manitoba and Saskatchewan. They travel with the seasons in small bands along the multitude of rivers and lakes in their vast territory in search of caribou, moose, BEAR, beaver and other game, fish, wildfowl and wild plants.

A SIOUAN WOMAN (above) in ceremonial costume displays her most precious possession: an elaborate necklace of dentalium shells, beads and silver coins.

DENTALIUM SHELLS (KARUK) represent an important symbol of wealth across the continent. Dentalium is a small, tusk-shaped mollusc that lives along the Pacific Coast from Alaska to California. The shells have been an important trade item in much of North America for thousands of years; the most desired variety was the pure white *Dentalium pretiosum* or "precious dentalium".

Dentalium Shell (Pisivava) lived alone in Upriver Ocean. He bore many young and, as they continued to grow, he decided to convert them into wealth for the people who were to come. He made strings from iris fibres and arranged the dentalia in necklaces of five sizes, the largest being the most valuable. To dress the shells up, he took the skin of a red-bellied snake, pulled it over them and decorated the top with a woodpecker crest. Then he made purses out of elk-

horn, deerskin and turtle-shell. With the necklaces finished, he created a human village out of his hair and instructed the people how to use the shells as a form of money – for buying women, paying blood money (compensation for murdered relatives) and gambling.

DEVIL'S TOWER, a large, grey volcanic core composed of igneous rock hardened into massive vertical columns and exposed by erosion, rises to a height of more than 366 m (1,200 feet) above the Belle Fourche River valley in northeast Wyoming. This striking monolith is held sacred by all the tribes of the region, including the KIOWA, ARAPAHO, SHOSHONI, CROW, CHEYENNE and Lakota SIOUX.

The Kiowa name, Tso-aa, or tree rock, relates to a story of its origin. Seven young girls were playing outside their village when a BEAR attacked them. They fled back towards the village, but had to take refuge on a small rock, and, as the bear came closer, they prayed to the rock to save them. The rock began to grow upwards until the girls were out of reach of the bear, who scratched in vain at the sides. The rock grew so high that the girls were pushed into the sky, where they became the seven stars now known as the PLEIADES.

DEVIL'S TOWER is a volcanic mass, one of its most striking aspects being its enormous ribs, formed from the cooling of the magma. They stand out starkly in late afternoon sunlight.

E

DIRTY BOY is the protagonist of a widespread theme involving the failure of people to appreciate true worth. He is commonly a boy so unattractive that most people shun him but, when someone treats him kindly, he transforms into a handsome young man, who returns the generosity shown him through his spiritual powers.

In a *BLACKFOOT* story cycle, Dirty Boy (also called Found-in-the-Grass) began life as *LODGE BOY*. He was one of two monster-slaying brothers. When his brother, Thrown Away, climbed a tree into the upper world and disappeared, Lodge Boy declined into the pathetic and unappealing Dirty Boy. A kindly old woman took him in and made him arrows, with which he won a shooting contest for the daughter of the chief. As his spirit grew stronger, he proved himself in further tests of strength and prowess, and grew into a handsome man. After saving his tribe by gathering up buffalo and ensuring their continued prosperity, he rose into the sky where he joined his brother in the constellation we now call Castor and Pollux.

DJILÁKONS
see *WEEPING WOMAN*.

DJOKÁBESH (*MONTAGNAIS, NASKAPI*), who figures in one of the first North American myths to be recorded (in the Jesuit Relations of 1634, by Father Paul le Jeune), is a *CULTURE HERO* and monster-slayer. In one of his exploits, he killed a monstrous *BEAR* that had eaten his mother. Unlike many roaming heroes, Djokábesh kept close to home, returning to his sister after each adventure. She had her own heroic qualities, once rescuing him when he was swallowed by a fish.

DOG HUSBAND (Iglulik *INUIT*) is a narrative theme that resolves the problem of how to maintain the integrity of the mythic world after human beings and animals are separated. This particular version also explains the origins of non-Inuit groups.

A father, frustrated by a daughter who would have no husband, cursed her by ordering her to marry his dog. A man soon appeared wearing a dog amulet, and married her. He was a dog in human form. The woman became pregnant and gave birth to a large litter – half of them human beings and the other half dogs. Since the dog-husband could not hunt like other Iglulik husbands, the woman's father had to provide meat. Because this went against all proper conduct, he resolved to kill his son-in-law. One day, the dog-husband swam from the father's camp with the meat, but it was weighed down with stones, and he drowned. Angry at her father for the curse that had caused this unnatural marriage in the first place, the woman called on her dog-children to kill the father. They mauled him, but he escaped and ceased to bring her food. With no one to supply meat, the young woman transformed her clothing (and/or her boots) into boats and sent the children out into the world to fend for themselves.

To the Inuit, these dog and human children became the ancestors of Indians (or spirits) and white people.

DOGRIB see *DENE*.

DJOKÁBESH killed a bear that had eaten his mother. Bears often feature as fierce adversaries in North American myths.

DREAMS are an essential aspect of a person's social identity and spiritual growth. They may have great import, especially at times of crisis or transition. At the birth of a child, a parent or elder may provide a name given in a dream; a youth undergoing the transition to adulthood may be expected to dream the presence of a guardian spirit; and dreams may guide people through hunting, travel, warfare or other important cultural events. *SHAMANS* use dreams as a means of gaining wisdom and understanding, using their experience, just as modern psychologists do, to help resolve problems in daily life. As the dream world is the world of spirits, it involves powerful forces that the dreamer must always respect; to ignore or misuse the wisdom of dreams can be dangerous.

DUNNE-ZA see *BEAVER*.

EAGLES, as large birds of prey with a commanding presence and the ability to soar high into the sky, are often associated with militaristic power and great hunting ability.

To the *WICHITA*, eagles were created when the father of *CULTURE HERO* Young-Boy-Chief (Waiksedia), weary of conflicts, asked the people of his village to abandon their village and their human forms. Some families turned into birds, others into animals of the forests and plains. For his part, the old chief poured a gourd of water over the fire in his lodge; as the steam and smoke enveloped his family,

SHAMANS USE dreams and trances to take them into the spirit world. In this Alaskan Inuit carving, a shaman sits in a trance, accompanied by two animal-like spirit helpers. The drum he uses to conjure the spirits lies beside him.

including Young-Boy-Chief, they rose into the sky as eagles. The *HOPI* relate how Eagle helped *COYOTE* steal a box of light – the sun and the moon – from the *KACHINAS*, while the *CROW* tribe associate eagles, especially bald-headed ones, with thunder. In *INUIT* beliefs, eagles dwell in the land above the sky, and so *SHAMANS* may place eagle down on the tops of ceremonial staffs during hunting rituals, to aid the hunters in their quest for game. For a *TUSKEGEE* creation myth, see *COUNCIL OF ANIMALS*.

THE EAGLE, largest of the hunting birds, soars high in the sky, scanning the landscape below with a keen vision that can spot the smallest of prey. Its size, strength and sharp senses make it one of the most powerful of the animal beings.

LANDSCAPES OF MEMORY

THE HEROIC EVENTS OF CREATION AND TRANSFORMATION do not depend only on the recollection of ancient traditions. They live on in the shape of the land itself: every towering rock or twist in a river records the acts of the culture heroes who changed the earth as they lived on it. In some places, the marks of creation are still fresh. Thus, the Choctaw can still gaze upon the very

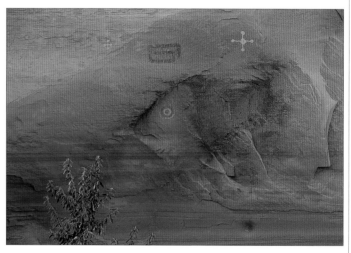

place they emerged, a mound called Nanih Waiya, near present-day Philadelphia, Mississippi. Other land forms preserve individual supernatural acts. The Penobscot, for example, can speak of a time when Gluskap killed a moose at Moose-tchick, for the bones and entrails of this giant creature are still visible around Bar Harbor, Maine. The story-teller's landscape also provides an effective mental map of a tribal homeland, coloured and textured with the places where supernatural events occurred (the ability to visualize environmental detail was crucial for people who often had to travel great distances over vast, trackless environments during their seasonal rounds). Since aboriginal people intertwine oral tradition and geography in this way, they still have a spiritual hold on their lost lands, a bond that they can verify and renew as long as those lands exist.

ANCIENT ROCKS (left) seem to bear the weight of eternity on their weathered heads. These pink granite domes thrust above the dry lands of central Texas, near a formation known as the Enchanted Rock. By night, the rock seems to recoil from the coolness of the air, for it emits strange cracking sounds, like voices from the depths of the earth.

A FISH (above) emerges from the jagged scars of a weathered layer of sandstone on the face of a cliff in Canyon de Chelly, Arizona. Aboriginal artists saw the natural earth as a place of transformation, where the essence of the ancestor creators remained, hidden in stone. With a touch of paint or some carving, these beings emerge, creating a place of worship for generations to come.

THE ROCKS (left) that form the skeletal structure of the earth are alive, as they have distinctive shapes and substance, exhibit change and decay, and hold within them the memories of the events of creation. In a small clearing in the woods of Pennsylvania, near the Delaware River, a host of weathered rocks carries a strange quality that made them sacred to the Unami and Munsee people who once lived here – when they are struck, they give off a bright, ringing sound. Wherever they are found, ringing rocks serve to confirm the subtle powers of even the most inanimate of earthly objects.

A GREAT SERPENT (right) was fashioned more than 2,000 years ago by the people of the Adena or Hopewell cultures, on a narrow promontory above Brush Creek, in Adams County, Ohio. The mound, built up with yellow clay and stones, is 440 m (400 yards) long. The serpent's tail is coiled, and it appears to be holding an egg in its mouth. Serpents figure in mythologies across the world, as they have the extraordinary power, reflected in their unique locomotion on the physical plane, to move between the surface of the earth and the underworld abodes of the spirits.

A PLACE (left) with great spiritual power may be marked by something startling, unexpected, that seems to remove it from the surrounding landscape. In the broad, flat prairies of Saskatchewan, there is an island of golden sand that rises into dunes covering 190,000 ha (470,000 acres). Here in the Great Sandhills, the Plains Cree believe that the Memekweciwak, or little people, dwell, making the chipped-stone artefacts that people still find along its margins.

F

EARTH DIVER is a *CREATION* theme, in which the earth is shaped from mud that an animal retrieves from the depths of the primeval waters. It has continuous distribution throughout Europe, Asia and most of North America. While most narratives keep to the conventional story of struggle by various animals to reach the bottom of the ocean and retrieve the mud (see *COUNCIL OF ANIMALS*), a northern Alaskan version has *RAVEN* diving under the water, spearing a clod of earth and raising it to the surface. And the *YAKIMA* peoples relate the story of Wheememeowah, the Great Chief Above, who completes the task himself, scooping mud from the shallows. For an Algonquian version, see *WISAKEDJAK*.

EARTH-MAKER is a creator who is found in the stories of several different tribal groups.

The *MAIDU* say that he floated on the primeval waters with *OLD MAN COYOTE*, and that the two of them decided to make land. They floated until they found what appeared to be a bird's nest (it was Meadowlark's nest). First they stretched the nest out to the rim of the world using ropes, then they painted it with blood, so that all kinds of creatures would be born (some rocks are still blood-red today, as proof of this event). By stretching it even further, they made it big enough to travel in. Earth-maker then went around making creatures, countries and languages, while Coyote maintained the ropes. When there is an earthquake, the people know that it is Coyote trying to stretch the world a little more.

The *PIMA* Earth-maker created people out of clay, but they were misshapen, and, after arguing with *ELDER BROTHER*, he sank into the earth. The *WINNEBAGO* relate that Earth-maker, after creating the earth, made *HARE* in the image of a man, and sent him into the world where he was born of a virgin. He

later founded the *MIDEWIWIN* society in order to secure human immortality.

ECHO (*UTE*) figures in an origin story that combines ribald humour with theorizing about a mysterious natural phenomenon.

Echo was a jealous, demanding woman who kidnapped Dove's child and raised him to be her husband. One day, the young man was out hunting when he came upon his mother. She was overjoyed to see him again, and they devised a plan so that he could escape from Echo. The next time he killed a buffalo, he piled the meat high in a cedar tree, forcing his wife to devise a way to get it down. While Echo struggled with the meat, the youth and his mother put a tree stump in his bed and ran away. When Echo returned with the meat, she saw the outline of her husband in the bed and, thinking she saw his erect penis above the blanket, had intercourse. When she discovered the ruse, she rushed after the two, who had flown up to his grandfather's home on a cliff. The grandfather, Rattlesnake, hid them outside the entrance to his cave and crawled back into the darkness. When Echo entered the cave, she saw an erect penis in the dim light and began to have intercourse. As she did, the cave got smaller and smaller, until there was just enough room for Rattlesnake to escape, leaving Echo trapped forever in the cliff.

ELDER BROTHER (*PIMA*), Siuuhu, was a son of sky and earth and the creator of the Hohokam (a prehistoric culture that disappeared *c.* 1450). After molesting some maidens at a puberty ceremony, he was killed. Four years later, he revived and followed the setting sun into the underworld. From there, he guided new people on to the earth, the present Pima, whom he led in battle against the Hohokam, driving them away. After creating the game animals and ceremonies necessary to propitiate the gods, he retired again to the underworld. He remains the patron of the war rite.

ESKIMO see *INUIT*.

ESTSÁNATLEHI
see *CHANGING WOMAN*.

FATHER SKY
see *MOTHER EARTH*.

A WESTERN DIAMONDBACK rattle-snake, featured in the Echo story, will shake its tail angrily to warn away predators.

FIRE is essential to human life, so its creation and control were among the most important tasks of *CULTURE HEROES*. Because of its value and its highly magical properties, fire was usually controlled by supernatural beings, and it was up to the heroes to steal it. Possessing fire is not enough, however. Fire-making tools must have the power to release the fire from the wood.

In a *YUROK* account, the animal heroes joined together to steal both fire and daylight from the sky people. At first the world was in darkness, and the animal people found this tiresome, so Megwom-ents (the dwarf food-giver) went to the sky and discovered that the sky people had abundant light. He came back to earth and then guided the *TRANSFORMER* Wohpe-kumeu, *EAGLE*, Pigeon, Sandpiper, Hummingbird and some other beings to the sky lodge where the light was kept. The sky people would not open the door, so *WOH-PEKUMEU* decided to impersonate a beautiful woman to get in. He tied his hair, took his blanket, a burden basket filled with acorns

FIRE is both terrible and wonderful – destructive as it rages through a northern California sequoia forest, but life-giving too, because the forest will revive with new vigour when the next spring arrives.

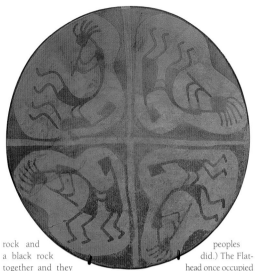

and salmon (they were actually pitch and alder bark) and a basket dipper, and easily gained entrance. Inside, the sky people were feasting, and he saw two baskets hanging, one holding fire and the other daylight. The revellers took no notice of him and, when they had finished their meal, they left him there alone (it was night, and they were busy with the night sky). Just before daylight, Wohpekumeu stole the baskets, but the sky people discovered the theft and pursued him. They had almost caught him when he gave the baskets to Eagle, who carried them further, and they were then passed in succession to Pigeon, Hummingbird, Sandpiper and, finally, Water Ant, who escaped into the water. When the sky people abandoned the chase, Water Ant came out of the water, daylight flooded the land, and he breathed the fire out of his mouth on to a willow tree – which is why fire drills are always made from willow.

The heroes in a *SANPOIL* version must make some sort of ladder to get into the sky, so they try to shoot an arrow into it and then make a chain of arrows down to the ground. All the animals fail except Woodpecker, who made his bow and arrows from superior materials – the bow of an elk rib, arrows from service-berry bushes and eagle feathers, and the points from flint (which he obtained by inducing Flint Rock and Hard Rock to fight). With the chain made, the animals bring the fire from the sky, and Horsefly and Hummingbird carry it to all parts of the Sanpoil country.

In the Yurok and Sanpoil narratives, culture heroes brought fire to the earth. In a *DENA* story it was humans that invented fire-making, spurred on by the selfish actions of a trickster. Long ago, when people had no fire, they watched *CROW* simply reach into the water and hook out burning coals, but they could never duplicate the feat. Then one day a boy struck a white rock and a black rock together and they sparked. He lit some grass, but the spark always died. Then another boy made a bow drill and surrounded the tip with the dried, rotten heartwood of a birch (punk). When he created a spark (a glowing coal), he lifted it with a bone knife into the grass, and it burned.

FLAT PIPE, the sacred *PIPE* of the *ARAPAHO*, is central to tribal identity. It is imbued with powerful *MEDICINE* and so must always be wrapped in a bundle and protected by a pipe-keeper.

Flat Pipe is, in essence, the force that created Arapaho culture. Its role is only revealed in the Flat Pipe ceremony, but several simplified accounts are recorded. Flat Pipe (the pipe is personified) floated on four sticks on the primeval waters. He bade the animals dive down into the waters and retrieve mud so that he could use it to make land, and finally Duck succeeded. There was not sufficient clay, however, so Turtle went down and got enough for Flat Pipe to create the earth.

THE FLATHEAD tribe are hunters, fishers and gatherers. They speak a Salishan language closely related to that of their northwestern neighbours, the Kalispel. (They were so named by whites under the misapprehension that they flattened their heads, as some coastal peoples did.) The Flathead once occupied much of the interior Plateau in western Montana and Idaho. After giving up their rights to this land in the Hellgate Treaty of 1855, they joined other Salish and Kootenay tribes on the Flathead Reservation in western Montana. Two unrelated tribes, the *CHINOOK* and *CHOCTAW*, were once also called Flatheads earlier in the historic period.

FLINT (*IROQUOIS*) is the evil one of *TWIN* brothers born to the daughter of *WOMAN-WHO-FELL-FROM-THE-SKY*. While Sapling, the good twin, transformed the landscape, slew monsters and created culture, Flint, with the aid of his grandmother, attempted to undo the good. Sapling created animals, but Flint kept them in a cave, and Sapling had to release them. Flint attempted to build an ice bridge to the land of the monsters, so that they could cross over and kill humans, but Sapling sent Bluebird to frighten Flint, and the ice melted. The flint (chert) used to make weapons is believed to be drops of Flint's blood, shed in fights with his brother.

FLUTE LURE is a mythological story-type in which the sound of a flute or other wood instrument plays a significant part. In a moralistic *PAPAGO* story, an outcast woman who has spent her life

struggling painfully through the mountains, used music (the sound of the flute) as a seductive device. She gave birth to *TWIN* boys who – magically – matured quickly and, to help them get married, she showed them how to make flutes from canes, so they could lure Buzzard's two daughters. After marrying the daughters, they went to visit Buzzard, but were killed by his henchman, Blue Hawk.

FLYING (OR ROLLING) HEADS feature as monsters in many oral traditions. For the *IROQUOIS*, the disembodied Flying Head is a creature of storms, four times as tall as the tallest man. Its thick skin is so matted with hair that no weapon can pierce it. The head has huge fangs, and two vast bird wings growing out of its cheeks, enabling it to fly.

THE MOON, the mother of twin boys in a Blackfoot account of creation, is beheaded for falling in love with a rattlesnake. Now a monstrous flying head, she chases the boys, but they will be saved when mountains spring up to protect them.

G

FLYING SHIELDS (*HOPI*) were made from woven cotton, and were used by supernatural beings for transportation.

FOAM WOMAN (*HAIDA*) was one of two mythic mothers of the Haida moieties (halves), into which the society was divided (the other was *WEEPING WOMAN*). Foam Woman was the ancestor of the Raven *CLANS*, and appeared at the time of the world flood. She had 20 breasts, ten on each side, and at each breast she nursed the future grandmother of one of the Raven families.

FOUND-IN-THE-GRASS
see *DIRTY BOY*.

THE FOX (Mesquaki), or Red Earth People, are an Algonquian tribe who ranged widely in the prairies west of Lake Michigan, where they hunted, fished, gathered and grew maize (corn), beans and other crops in season. After being nearly exterminated in the early 18th century, they joined forces with their traditional allies, the Sauk (or Sac), forming the Sac and Fox Nation. They removed to Iowa in 1804 after an unjust treaty gave them a pittance – about $2,000 and an annuity in goods worth approximately $1,000 – in exchange for all their lands east of the Mississippi (a large part of present-day Illinois, Missouri, and Wisconsin). In 1827, they rebelled

KEOKUK, Sauk and Fox chief, c. 1848. Unlike the heroic resistance leader Black Hawk, Keokuk co-operated with the whites, and was eventually responsible for signing away most tribal land.

when the Federal government decided to remove all native people from Illinois. The Sauk leader Ma-ka-tai-me-she-kia-kiak (Black Sparrow Hawk), known popularly as Black Hawk, and his people (warriors, women and children) were eventually crushed in 1832 at the Massacre of Bad Axe, on the Mississippi River. The Sauk chief Keokuk eventually signed away all but 16 ha (40 acres) of the remaining tribal lands. In 1857, the survivors purchased a small plot of land along the Iowa River in central Iowa, and they remained there after the Sauk were forced to move to Kansas in 1861. This land, which is not a government-controlled reservation, is called the Mesquaki Indian Settlement.

THE GABRIELINO, speaking an Uto-Aztecan language, was a small hunting and gathering tribe that occupied lands in southern California around present-day Los Angeles. They were especially skilled deep-sea fishers, taking their plank boats well offshore in search of sea lions, seals, otters and a wide variety of fish, including swordfish, halibut and tuna. They were once considered extinct, but the resurgence of pride in Indian identity caused a number of Gabrielinos to reassert their tribal affiliation. They have no land base, but several groups are actively trying to regenerate their traditional culture.

GAHÉ (*APACHE*) are the supernatural beings who are represented by gahé dancers (corresponding to the Pueblo *KACHINA* dancers). The Chiricahua Apache believe that the gahé live inside certain mountains and wear costumes and decorate their faces in ways that Chiricahua learn through visionary experience,

and subsequently recreate in their dances. The gahé dancers appear at curing rituals and at girls' puberty rites. The gahé also act as protectors of the Chiricahua people. One narrative describes how they rescued an Apache war party, equipped only with traditional weapons, that was being pursued by Mexican cavalry. A man prayed to the gahé of a nearby mountain, who poured out and surrounded the soldiers. They opened a cave in the rocks and drove them all inside, then closed it forever. It is said that one can still see the soldiers' shoes piled up at the mouth of the cave.

GLUSKAP is the principal *CULTURE HERO* and *TRANSFORMER* of northeastern Algonquian coastal peoples, also known as Glooskap. He is similar in essence and character to a hero of Algonquian tribes in northeastern woodlands, *NANABUSH*, and to a hero of Algonquian tribes south of the Great Lakes, known as *WISAKEDJAK*. Like Wisakedjak, Gluskap has no clearly defined animal attributes.

Gluskap's origins are obscure, since most narratives focus on his exploits. In a Christianized myth of the western *ABENAKI*, he formed himself out of the dust left over from the creation of Adam.

In a recent *MICMAC* version, lightning created Gluskap when one bolt struck the sand and formed the image of a human body, and a second strike gave him life. At first, he was stuck to the ground

THE GAHÉ, or spirits of the mountains, are represented here by Apache dancers. The dancers are also sometimes called Mountain Spirit Dancers or Fire Dancers. They dance to ward off evil spirits and illness during the Apache girls' puberty ceremonies.

with his head facing the rising sun, his feet towards the setting sun, and his arms pointing north and south. After watching animals, birds and plants thrive around him, he asked Nisgam (Sun) to free him. At that moment a third bolt of lightning raised him to his feet so that he could walk the earth.

Gluskap explored the land in all directions, travelling west until he came to an ocean, south until the land narrowed and he could see an ocean on each side, and north to the land of ice and snow. Eventually he returned to the lands of his creation, and stayed there.

A *PENOBSCOT* story cycle captures some of his heroic deeds. He freed all the *HARES* of the world after fighting through blizzards when they were imprisoned by the Great Hare; he killed a monster frog that had drunk all the world's water, causing a drought; he rescued his brother Wolf from the serpent Atosis; and he tamed the giant wind bird (known to the *PASSAMAQUODDY* as Wuchowsen, or Wind-Blower, who sits on a great rock at the north end of the sky). Traces of his exploits can still be seen across the Atlantic region, from agates in the Minas Basin of Nova Scotia – jewels that he made for his grandmother's necklace – to mountains and rock outcrops all along the coast.

GREAT SPIRIT is the name commonly given to a singular creator. Such a being probably existed in the ancient beliefs of some tribes, but it is generally inconsistent with the spirit of egalitarianism and democracy that characterizes most tribal groups. It is likely that some creators of this type have emerged through the influence of Christianity.

GRIZZLY BEAR WOMAN (NEZ PERCE) exemplifies the unpredictable nature of BEARS, as benign foragers and fierce and aggressive adversaries, which makes them difficult beings to control in the spirit world.

The Nez Perce believe that when a woman becomes involved with a grizzly bear spirit, its strength overwhelms her, and she takes on its monstrous character. They relate the story of a young girl kidnapped from her family by bears. When her brother, Red-headed Woodpecker, found her after a long search, she complained that they mistreated her: she was degraded and humiliated in shocking ways – they forced her to eat naked, as was their custom, and they wiped their buttocks on her. To rescue her, Woodpecker gained entry to the bears' lodge by taking the form of a handsome

THE GREAT SPIRIT, or creator, is invoked by a warrior in a Plains Indian earthlodge. He lies beside the sacred fire beneath the smokehole which is open to the heavens. (PAINTING BY GEORGE CATLIN, C. 1830.)

youth. He ate with them (they hastily covered themselves in his presence) and then kept them up so late that they fell into a deep sleep. He then tied each one by its hair to a tent pole and set fire to the lodge. He urged his sister to flee, but, strangely, she asked him to wait and watch the bears burn. When the fire was over, she secretly picked up the bears' teeth from the ashes as they began the journey home. While they were walking home, the brother heard a growling noise behind him, and he discovered that his sister had changed into a bear. She began to chase him, hoping to catch and eat him, but he was saved by a group of women out digging roots. He took these women as his wives, and his sister was condemned to roam the forests in search of human prey.

THE GROS VENTRE, unaccountably given this name ("Big Bellies") by French explorers, call themselves Ah-ah-nee-nin, which

A GRIZZLY BEAR'S uncontrolled rage, when provoked, makes it one of the most dangerous of forest animals and feared by all the North American tribes.

means White Clay People. They are an Algonquian tribe, related to the ARAPAHO, who migrated long ago from the edge of the boreal forest near Lake Winnipeg to join other forest peoples on the Great Plains. After the introduction of the horse to North America, the Gros Ventre people began to specialize in buffalo-hunting, and they followed the vast herds across the broad plains of Montana and Saskatchewan. They eventually gave up their claims to their traditional territory in 1888, and were removed to a reservation at Fort Belknap, in Montana, which they share with the ASSINBOINE. They were traditionally allied with the BLACKFOOT and the SARCEE in the Blackfoot Confederacy.

THE HAIDA [Coastal, Island] occupy the Queen Charlotte Islands (Haida Gwaii) off the coast of British Columbia and small section of the Alaska mainland. Along with their northern neighbours, the TLINGIT, they speak a Na-Dene language. As the warm Pacific waters teem with life, and the forests are deep and lush, the Haida obtained sufficient resources from fishing, hunting and gathering to support a social structure more typical of complex agricultural societies, with ranked social classes and private property. The exuberant outpouring of heraldic art strongly manifests the hierarchical nature of the society. Representations of the animal ancestors of CLANS and families are carved or painted on virtually all formal objects, including TOTEM POLES, house-fronts and

THE HAIDA inhabit the Queen Charlotte Islands. This 19th-century photograph shows how their cedar plank houses and totem poles followed the edge of the sea.

house support posts, masks, headdresses, boxes, dishes, basketry and many other material goods.

Both island and coastal Haida were subject to strenuous efforts by governments and missionaries to assimilate them, but they have kept much of their culture, and remain in the area of their original homelands. (See also TRANSFORMATION)

SPIRITS OF THE EARTH

THE EARTH IS INFUSED WITH SPIRITUAL ENERGY. When supernatural beings shaped the lands during the age of transformation, all material things had the potential to live as humans and animals do. Because of this legacy, aboriginal thinkers see the earth as a living spiritual realm where supernatural beings still reside. Every territory has its special places. A large hill near the junction of the Snake and Grande Ronde rivers (in present-day Idaho), for example, figures prominently in a Nez Perce fire story. Of the supernatural protagonists, Cedar, old and half dead, remained on the top of this hill for generations around the turn of the 20th century. The visual impact of this tree, craggy, ancient,

and etched against the sky, created a spiritual link that many other sacred places share. High mountains and prominent rock formations, caves and crevices, waterfalls and springs are all spirit dwellings. Whether the earthly spirits live, ever-watchful, above the land or are hidden away, to be suddenly encountered on a path or waterway, they always remain powerful, even dangerous, in their abodes.

A TALL BLOCK (left) of ancient sediment stands like a sentinel among the mountains along the border between Alberta and Montana. Because of its solitary, commanding presence, it is known as Chief Mountain. The Blackfoot regard it as a highly sacred place, where people may seek dreams and visions, and draw spiritual power.

THE DARK OPENING (above) of Danger Cave, in the western desert of Utah, looks over barren salt flats. The first humans to live here, 11,000 years ago, walked through grasslands and pine forest but, several thousand years later, the land had become too inhospitable to support them. To Native American people, such sites are sacred places, as they contain the spirits of all those ancestors who lived and died there.

MOUNTAINS (left) reach so high into the sky that the forces controlling the weather move among them. Here the snows cover the Sandia Mountains, near Albuquerque, New Mexico. Climbing to such heights is a journey into the realms of the spirit world, done carefully and with respect.

BEAVERHOUSE LAKE (below left), in northwestern Ontario, is dominated by a massive, domed granite formation resembling a beaver's lodge. At the highest point, reached by a steep climb up the cliffs, a single smear of red ochre indicates the site of a vision quest. It was an ideal spot, secluded and yet close to the sky and the immense sweep of the lake.

FANTASTIC WATER CREATURES (below), can be seen carved on a rock cliff along the shore of Sproat Lake, in Nootka territory on western Vancouver Island. They may have figured in mythological interpretations of the lake and its resources or in origin stories related to an important tribal ancestor.

AN ETHEREAL DAWN (right) breaks over brooding waters near the Lake of the Woods, Ontario. This view is from a large, square room cut by nature into a massive granite formation covered with red ochre rock paintings. The walls inside this strange opening are bare, suggesting that it was perhaps too filled with spirit power to be sullied by paint. Here, a shaman would have conducted rituals to obtain the visions and dreams necessary for contact with the manitous in the rocks and the waters below.

resplendent in a large, gold-trimmed cocked hat with great white plumes.

HASTSHIN (Jicarilla *APACHE*) were beings who existed in the beginning, when there was only Darkness, Water and Cyclone. They created the earth and the underworld, and then the sky.

HEROIC CHILDREN are very common characters in mythologies. They embody a range of cultural values common to most societies: innocence, which makes them closer than adults to an idealized spiritual condition; potential, in their energy for moral and spiritual growth as they mature; and continuity, in their significance as members of an emerging generation. Given their nearness to creation and its resources of spiritual power, it is not surprising that heroic children may mature unusually quickly, or are wise beyond their years. Heroic children are also an effective dramatic device, as there may be a great disparity between the child and its adversaries. They must often slay a host of fearsome monsters, for example, or undergo tests of character and determination, or outwit adults of a much higher social status, but perhaps fewer virtues. Children are naturally imbued with the promise of a better world, and perhaps this,

more than anything, makes their heroic deeds during the mythical age reasonable and appropriate. Examples of heroic children are *MUSP AND KOMOL*; *LODGE BOY AND THROWN AWAY*; *STAR BOY*; and Sweet Medicine (see under *HOOP-AND-POLE GAME*).

THE HIDATSA are a Siouan people who once lived along the Missouri River in western North Dakota. They had come from the woodlands and prairies south of the Great Lakes long ago, and their traditions say they emerged from Devil's Lake in eastern North Dakota. They were sophisticated horticulturalists, who not only grew corn (maize), squash and five varieties of beans, but practised seed selection and controlled plantings. They also hunted buffalo when necessary. After being distracted by the fur trade and severely reduced in the mid-19th century by smallpox and inter-tribal conflicts, induced by the westward spread of white culture, they joined other tribes on the Fort Berthold Reservation in North Dakota.

THE HOOP-AND-POLE GAME is a game with religious overtones, played across the continent. Players attempt to throw sharpened poles through a hoop. The enclosed space is generally divided into sections by twine or rawhide, and the score is calculated according to which section of the hoop the pole goes through.

The Northern *CHEYENNE* attribute the origins of the game to the *CULTURE HERO* Sweet Medicine. A young virgin of a good family bore a child after hearing a voice, for four nights in succession, telling her that a spirit man named Sweet Root

THE HAN (Han-Kutchin) are an Athapascan-speaking people who live in the boreal forests of eastern Alaska and adjoining parts of Yukon Territory in Canada. They live in isolated settlements along rivers and lakes, where they continue to pursue some of their traditional hunting and gathering activities, including moose hunting, salmon fishing and berry picking.

THE HARE tribe is a nomadic Athapascan hunting and gathering tribe concentrated northwest of Great Bear Lake on the northern edge of the boreal forests. They lived in small bands and travelled through their vast territory along the many rivers and lakes, subsisting on caribou, moose, deer, beaver and other small game, fish, wildfowl and seasonal berries and roots. Because of their remoteness, they have been able to retain many of their traditional ways.

HARES and rabbits figure in many oral traditions as *CULTURE HEROES* and *TRICKSTERS*. Great Hare (Winabojo, *NANABUSH*) is the principal culture hero of northeastern and Subarctic Algonquian cultures; and Hare (called Mastshingke, or rabbit, by the *OMAHA*) is a hero and trickster who delivers the Siouan peoples of the Great Plains from man-eating *BEARS*, rolling heads and other monsters.

Rabbit (Mahtigwess) is known to the *MICMAC* and *PASSAMAQUODDY* as a trickster with great magical powers. In a tale set during historic times, he throws a chip of wood into the water and transforms it into a three-masted ship, complete with coloured flags, three rows of heavy cannon and a crew – with himself as the captain,

would visit her. Shamed by her unexplained pregnancy, she abandoned the baby she delivered. An old woman nearby heard the baby's cries and took it home. She named the boy Sweet Medicine, because she found him where MEDICINE roots grew that helped make mothers' breast milk flow.

The boy grew unnaturally quickly and became a highly skilled hunter, even though still a child. Yet no one paid attention to him because he lived with an aged grandmother in a poor TEPEE. So he directed his grandmother to make a hoop wrapped with buffalo hide and prepare four cherry sticks. When she had done so, he began to throw the pointed sticks through the hoop. This new game attracted the people, and they gathered around. He threw the last stick, and when it went through the hoop, it changed into a fat buffalo calf. This calf was magical: no matter how much meat the people cut off, there was always more. This accounts for the promise in every hoop-and-pole game that the playing will ensure an abundance of buffalo.

A YOUNG HOPI girl wears her hair in the squash-blossom (or butterfly) style, indicating that she is available for marriage. After marriage, she will wear a simple braid.

THE HOPI [Hopituh Shi-nu-mu] are a western PUEBLO people who live in the area of Black Mesa in northeastern Arizona, surrounded by the territory of their regional rivals, the NAVAJO. They speak an Uto-Aztecan language, which reveals a southern affiliation quite distinct from that of the Atha-pascan Navajos. They lived in large community houses, built of stone or *adobe* (mud bricks), in towns established well before the historic period. The Hopi practised the small-scale horticulture typical of southern tribes, growing corn (maize), beans, squash and cotton. Through careful selection of their corn crops, they developed a plant with a tap root long enough to endure the arid conditions of their fields, and they also selected varieties in their four sacred colours – red, white, blue and yellow. They expanded into cattle-ranching after the arrival of Europeans.

HORSES transformed native cultures, practically and spiritually, during the historic period, especially in the Great Plains. They escaped into the wild in 1540, during the first Spanish expedition into the Southwest. Numbers increased dramatically when the Spanish retreated after the Pueblo rebellion in 1680. The use of the horse quickly spread from the PUEBLO across the deserts and grasslands of the continent; records of French traders in Kansas indicate that the CHEYENNE were using the horse by 1745. The Indians had no word for "horse", so they created one out of words they used for other animals: for example, Elk Dog, Spirit Dog, Sacred Dog or Moose Dog. As all religions strive to account for mysteries within the specific experience of the culture, there are origin stories that regard the horse as a gift of the supernaturals.

According to the BLACKFOOT, the CULTURE HERO Long Arrow brought the first horses to the tribe. Long Arrow was an unfortunate orphan boy: deaf, treated like a mangy dog and unloved by everyone but his sister. When the people broke camp, they simply abandoned him, but a kindly old chief named Good Running eventually adopted him. The boy recovered

BEFORE THE WHITE MAN divided up the vast open plains with barbed wire, the Indian people let their horses range wild, catching and taming them as they were needed. (19TH-CENTURY PAINTING BY GEORGE CATLIN.)

his hearing, learned to speak and eventually grew up to be a fine hunter. When he asked his adopted father how he could repay him for his kindness, the chief told him that there was talk of powerful spirit people living at the bottom of a faraway lake. They had mysterious animals to do their work – swift and strong and bigger than elk, but able to carry burdens like dogs. He called them Pono-Kamita (Elk Dogs). Every fourth generation, young warriors had gone in quest of one of these wonderful creatures, but they had never returned.

Long Arrow took up the challenge and, after a long journey and encounters with many spirits, found a giant lake surrounded by snowy peaks and waterfalls of ice. After falling asleep in a meadow, he was awoken by a beautiful spirit boy-child, who took Long Arrow to his grandfather's lodge at the bottom of the lake. The grandfather lived in a large TEPEE of tanned buffalo hide, decorated with images of two strange animals in vermilion paint and with a kingfisher perched on top. Since Long Arrow had braved the journey into the depths of the lake, the grandfather rewarded him with one of the Elk Dogs. When he discovered that the grandfather himself was an Elk Dog and the master of these animals, Long Arrow asked for three things:

the grandfather's rainbow-coloured quilled belt, his black MEDICINE robe and a herd of Elk Dogs. If he wore the robe, Long Arrow would be able to prevent the animals from running away, and if he learned the dance song and prayers carried by the belt, he would always maintain the animals' respect. He then caught one of the Elk Dogs with a magic rope woven from the hair of a white buffalo bull, and rode home with the herd, never looking back along the way. He brought the animals to his tribe, and they never again had to struggle on foot to move their travois or hunt the buffalo. (See also THE STRANGERS)

47

I

THE HUPA

THE HUPA are an Athapascan people of hunters and gatherers who once lived in the Hoopa Valley along the lower Trinity River in northwest California. Their most important foods were salmon and acorns, both abundant at different times during the year. Like the Northwest Coast peoples, they had concepts of wealth and private property, related to fishing grounds and oak groves. The tribe now occupies a small reservation within its ancient homeland.

HURON see under WYANDOT.

IKTOMI (SIOUX) is a TRICKSTER, the first son of INYAN. His mischief figures in a Dakota Sioux CREATION account. Waziya (Old Man) and his wife Wakanka, who lived beneath the earth, had a daughter, Ite, who was married to Tate (the Wind). Iktomi convinced her parents that, if they helped him play a prank on the other gods, Ite's beauty would rival that of Hanwi (the Moon). Iktomi gave Ite a charm that caused her to dwell more and more on her appearance and less and less on her sons (the Four Winds). Then, at a feast of the gods, Ite captivated Wi (the Sun) so much that he gave up his wife Hanwi's seat to her. Hanwi was humiliated. After a council, Skan (the Sky, and judge of gods and spirits) ruled that the Sun would lose the comfort of his wife, the Moon; he would rule in the day and she at night, and whenever they were together she would cover her face in shame.

IN THE JUMP DANCE, or Redheaded Woodpecker Dance, a world renewal ceremony, Hupa dancers wear headdresses of red woodpecker crests edged with deerskin and topped by a fringe of deer hair, large strings of dentalium shells, and deerskin robes, worn as kilts. The function of the straw-stuffed cylinders they carry is no longer known by modern Hupa. (PHOTOGRAPH BY E. S. CURTIS, C. 1896.)

THE INUIT [Alaskan, Central, Greenland], commonly known to outsiders as Eskimos (a pejorative Algonquian term meaning "eaters of raw meat"), occupy the Arctic regions of the continent, from Alaska to Greenland. They spread by sea from Siberia much later than other North American peoples, perhaps 5,000 years ago.

Inuit culture is relatively uniform, as all its peoples speak Eskimo-Aleut languages and share a harsh, mainly treeless environ-

A GROUP OF INUIT ELDERS are wearing labrets (lip plugs). Alaskan and Mackenzie Delta Inuit carved these plugs in ivory, stone or other materials, and wore them as decorations.

ment bordering the North Pacific Ocean, the Bering Sea and the Arctic Ocean. These regions all experience short summers and very long, dark and cold winters. Cultural differences relate to the proximity of Inuit groups to other peoples, including ALEUTS and North American Indians, and to variations in habitat, from the extreme northern polar regions to the edges of the boreal forest.

Alaskan groups include the Kodiak Island peoples, the Tikigaq and the Iñupiat. The Kobuk are a band of Iñupiat who live in western Alaska. The Nunamiut are an inland people subsisting mainly on caribou.

Central groups, occupying the Arctic mainland and island regions of Canada, include the Mackenzie, the Copper, the Netsilik, the Iglulik and the Baffin Island Inuit. They are the classic "Eskimos", who lived in igloos during the long Arctic winters and hunted for seal at breathing holes in ice floes, travelling by dog team and sled. The Caribou are an inland people who hunted caribou and fished the freshwater lakes and rivers northeast of Hudson Bay.

The Greenland people include the Polar Inuit, who live along the Greenland coast north of Baffin Island. (See also NEW GODS, NEW MYTHOLOGIES, THE DARK SIDE)

INYAN (SIOUX), or Rock, is the ancestor of all things. Inyan was a soft, unformed mass, imbued with power, but alone. So he opened his veins and created Maka, the earth. As his blood was blue, it flowed over Maka, making the sky and the waters. The loss of blood made Inyan shrink and become hard, and he lost his power.

THE IOWA (Paxoje), a Siouan culture, originated in the region south of the Great Lakes, but eventually joined the tribal movement west as buffalo hunting became a major form of subsistence. Their tribal name is Paxoje, which means Dusty Noses, but they refer to themselves in English as Ioway. During the 1870s, the tribe split in two: some members accepted individual allotments near the Missouri River along the Kansas–Nebraska border (now a reservation) while others travelled to Indian Territory (now Oklahoma) and lived on common land. The latter group gained a reservation in 1883 but, after the Dawes Act of 1887, the government opened it up to white settlers as part of the 1889 Oklahoma Land Run. Today they control approximately 80 ha (200 acres) of Federal trust lands, scattered in north-central Oklahoma. The two groups are now separate and, like all other Native American nations, are threatened by assimilation – through decline in the number of native speakers, a small and fragmented land base, intermarriage with whites and the ideological and economic impact of the dominant American culture.

IQIASUAK (Nunamiut INUIT) was a man who willingly transformed himself into a caribou

K

because he was lazy and could not face the responsibilities of human life. He was eventually killed by an equally lazy hunter who failed to butcher him properly, forgetting to detach the skull from the atlas vertebrae. This imprisoned his soul in the skull, and he could only watch helplessly as the spirits of the other caribou escaped so that they could be reincarnated. Eventually, another hunter came along and, attracted by the rack of antlers, detached the vertebrae, so freeing Iqiasuak's soul.

THE IROQUOIS [Haudenosaunee] are five Iroquoian-speaking tribes – Mohawk, Oneida, Onondaga, Cayuga and Seneca – who controlled a large territory east of Lakes Ontario and Erie in the north-east woodlands. They were horticulturalists, who raised corn (maize), squash and beans, supplemented by hunting and gathering, in the temperate open woodlands of the region. Their habitations were distinctive communal longhouses, made of bent saplings covered with bark, which extended up to 91 m (300 feet).

In the 17th century, they were allied in a confederacy given supernatural sanction by the unifying exploits of the CULTURE HERO

A CARVED WOODEN MASK with braided horsehair was used by members of the False Face Society of the Iroquois during curing (world renewal) ceremonies. Dancers wore such masks to invoke the spirits and gain protection for the tribe.

CARIBOU (genus rangifer), which feature in the Iquiasak story, live in the tundra and boreal forest margins of Canada and Alaska.

DEGANAWIDA. The Tuscarora, a related tribe occupying present-day North Carolina, joined the alliance in the 18th century, creating the Six Nations Confederacy. The alliance fell apart during the American Revolution, as the tribes could not agree which side to support. Many Iroquois settled after the war on the Six Nations Reserve near Brantford, Ontario, while the rest moved to the Buffalo Creek Reservation in New York State. Each group has its own confederacy council. (See also DEATH AND AFTERLIFE, THE STRANGERS)

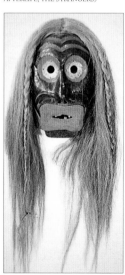

JESUS CHRIST (Chiricahua *APACHE*) and his Resurrection have influenced an account of the departure of the culture hero CHILD-OF-THE-WATER from the earth. At the end of his journeys, Child-of-the-Water visited his mother's birthplace, where he was killed and put in a cave blocked by a big stone; he had a large spear wound in his left side. His mother, WHITE-PAINTED WOMAN, cried outside the cave, and heard him say that he would see her again. On the third day he rose into the sky and, when the people moved back the big stone, the cave was empty.

JESUS THE TRAVELLER (interior *SALISH*) is a substitute for the traditional TRANSFORMER, Hwan, in one CHEHALIS story-teller's narrative. Jesus the Traveller teaches people to make wedges and mauls for splitting wood, better ways to catch salmon, transforms monsters, and drops fish bones into rivers, creating salmon, suckers and trout.

KACHINAS (*HOPI*) are the gods who live unseen and participate in human affairs. They are similar to spirits of the dead, for the Hopi believe that those who have led a proper life come back as Kachinas. They usually reside at springs and travel about in the clouds, and, because of their association with water, the people pray to them for rain. Hopis say that they must represent the Kachinas by masked dancers and votive dolls because the real Kachinas have abandoned them, the result of Hopi transgressions.

KÁNEKELAK (*KWAKIUTL*) is a character who figures in a variation of the widespread mythological theme of HEROIC CHILDREN.

Kánekelak and his younger brother had selfish parents who mistreated them. While the children starved, the parents feasted on ever larger catches of salmon. When Kánekelak discovered their

secret, he threw his father into the air, turning him into a heron, and transformed his mother into a red-headed woodpecker. To protect his brother, now named Only One, he built him an enormous house, left him four whales to eat, and went out into the world. He slew monsters, transformed the dangerous animal people into the animals of today,

KACHINA DANCERS carve small replicas of the kachina gods called tihu and give them to females, especially girls nearing marriage. The effigies are invested with Kachina spirit, so they are kept in the house, where they are attached to the walls or rafters.

met the ancestors of the Kwakiutl CLANS, and at last returned to the house to find that his brother had long ago starved to death, leaving only a pile of dry bones. Kánekelak revived Only One with the water of life and then sent him to live out his days in the north, while he himself retired to the south.

KARARIWARI see *POLARIS*.

THE KARUK (Karok) people are a Hokan-speaking tribe who occupied the central part of the Klamath River basin in northwestern California, subsisting by salmon-fishing, hunting and gathering. They gradually dispersed under pressure from incoming white settlers, losing almost all their territory. Today, they have a very small land base in the region, but continue to pursue aspects of their traditional culture.

KATS (*TLINGIT*) is the protagonist in a Tékwedi *CLAN* crest origin myth. Kats, a member of the Tékwedi clan, married a grizzly-*BEAR* woman, and they had both human children and bear children. When he refused to feed his bear children, the bears killed him, and the Tékwedi, in response, claimed the grizzly crest to display on their *TOTEM POLES* and houses.

KERES see *PUEBLO*.

THE KICKAPOO people are an Algonquian tribe who originated in the woodlands south of the lower Great Lakes. Here, they carried on a typical seasonal round of hunting, fishing, gathering and some horticulture. In 1819, many bands of Kickapoo were pushed out of their homelands, between the Wabash and Illinois rivers in Illinois and Indiana, to accommodate veterans of the War of 1812. Several bands resisted, however. Among them, the chief Mecina and his band fought back, but they were forced across the Mississippi by the military after months of fighting. Another chief, Kennekuk (who was also a prophet, preaching a return to traditional ways), managed to resist peacefully until the end of the Black Hawk War in 1832. The forced migrations and dispersals scattered tribal groups across the states of Indiana, Illinois, Missouri and Texas.

KIOWA GIRLS and a baby are all prepared for an important ceremony. The girls wear fringed, painted deerskin, and the baby carrier is elaborately decorated with quillwork and trade beads.

By the turn of the 20th century, the Kickapoo were divided into two groups, one in Oklahoma, Texas and Mexico, the other in Kansas. The Kansas Kickapoo, removed there from Illinois in 1832, occupy a reservation that the government gradually reduced from 310,000 to 8,100 ha (768,000 to 20,000 acres), less than half of it under tribal control. The Kickapoo to the south live on small land allotments. Although now politically separated, the tribes continue to maintain a common religion.

THE KIOWA tribe are a hunting and gathering people who speak a Kiowan-Tanoan language. They migrated to the southern plains from the mountainous regions to the northwest, near the headwaters of the Yellowstone River in present-day Montana, attracted by the vast buffalo herds. After fierce resistance to

THIS ANCIENT PETROGLYPH (rock carving) is said to represent the hunchbacked flute-player Kokopelli. It is located near Galisteo, New Mexico.

white settlement in the 1860s and 1870s, the survivors were removed to the Kiowa-Comanche-Apache Reservation in southwest Oklahoma but, in 1900, the government broke up this reservation and allotted less than 20 per cent of the land to the tribes. They continue to occupy these Federal trust lands.

KIVAS (*HOPI*) are semi-subterranean chambers, usually circular, used for ceremonies and as gathering places. In the kiva is the *SIPAPU*, the symbolic centre of the world. The kiva is a focus of community activity. *KACHINA* dancers practise there and hold dance performances, and the Flute and Snake societies (see *SECRET SOCIETIES*) hold meetings. Men and boys may weave there and make kachina dolls and bows and arrows, and women hold their own special rites.

A CIRCULAR MASONRY structure at Pueblo del Arroyo, Chaco Canyon, New Mexico. The Anasazi people, ancestors of modern Pueblo tribes, built the pueblo between c. 1065 and 1140. Although no evidence remains of use, the structure probably served as a kiva (a Hopi word meaning "ceremonial house").

KLAMATH See under *MODOC*.

KOKOPELLI (*PUEBLO*), the so-called humpbacked flute player, is widely represented in prehistoric rock art and on pottery. Since his phallus is often prominently displayed in such depictions, he is speculatively associated with fertility, and has become a popular symbol outside traditional native religion. Among the *HOPI* he has also become a contemporary *KACHINA*, associated with seduction, procreation and hunting.

KOMOL See under *MUSP*.

THE KOOTENAY (Kutenai), whose name means "water people", lived along the eastern flanks of the Columbia Plateau, to the east of the Rocky Mountains, where they fished for trout and sturgeon in the lakes and rivers, hunted elk, deer and other forest game, and gathered food plants in season. Linguists generally regard their language as an isolate (meaning that it is unconnected to any other known language group), but some theorize that it may possibly be related to Algonquian. The Kootenay now occupy small reservations and

allotments in southeast British Columbia and adjoining parts of Montana, Idaho and Washington.

KUTOYIS see *BLOOD CLOT*.

THE KWAKIUTL (Kwakwa-ka'wakw) are a Wakashan-speaking people who occupy northern Vancouver Island and the adjoining mainland. As inhabitants of the Pacific coast, with its rich diversity of deep-sea, coastal and inland food resources, the Kwakiutl developed a social structure more typical of a complex agricultural society, with ranked social classes and private property. They underwent the depredations typically suffered by tribes in the region, being decimated by smallpox and other diseases and harassed by missionaries. They remain, however, in parts of their original homeland and continue to pursue many of their traditional cultural practices, including a dramatic art style, expressed in the carving of *TOTEM POLES*, masks and other ceremonial objects, and elaborate ceremonials, all celebrating the mythological heroes and events of their past. (See also *THE DARK SIDE*)

KYÁLKO (*ZUNI*), the messenger god, brings to the people the story of emergence from out of the underworld every four years. He acts through the Kyálko impersonator, who recreates this central narrative as part of a young man's puberty ceremony.

KWAKIUTL artists create deeply carved and brightly painted wooden masks that lend great drama to the dances of the winter ceremonial season. This thunderbird headdress, dating to before 1920, is identified by its down-turned beak and horns. A dancer used it in the "Tsayeka" or red cedar bark dance series.

LAKOTA see *SIOUX*.

LANDSCAPE and the shape of the physical world reinforces the reality of traditional ideas about the past and acts as a permanent storage place for tribal memories.

When the Chiricahua *APACHE CULTURE HERO CHILD-OF-THE-WATER* killed a giant who was encased in four jackets of flint, the monster fell over four mountain ridges. The rocks still show where he fell – probably in the form of outcrops of flint (actually chert), which prehistoric peoples valued highly as a source of raw material for their tools. One can ride a horse through Child-of-the-Water's bones, and the ashes of the fire that he and his companion, Killer-of-Enemies, made when the giant disturbed them are still visible on the ground.

THE GRANITE MONOLITH of El Capitan in Yosemite National Park, California, stands like a massive sentinel at the entrance to the Yosemite Valley. Its sheer cliffs drop more than 915 m (3,000 feet). The effect is visually and spiritually overwhelming, making this an important part of the cultural landscape of the Sierra Miwok who settled here.

Mountains are very commonly the subject of origin stories. The *YOSEMITE* (Sierra Miwok) explain the origin of Tutokanula (today known as El Capitan, a large mountain in Yosemite National Park) as a supernatural event triggered by two young and curious adventurers who often ranged far from home. One day these boys found a new lake, so they decided to swim across to a large rock on the other side. They climbed the rock and fell asleep in the sun on the top, but, strangely, continued to sleep through the night and the next day, and for a long time after that. As they slept, the rock grew higher and higher until it became a huge granite mountain that brushed the sky. The boys eventually awoke to find themselves trapped. When the animals heard of the plight of the boys, they decided to try and save them. Each tried to jump to the mountain top: the mouse jumped a foot, the rat two feet, the raccoon higher, and the grizzly *BEAR* and mountain lion higher still, but none of them could succeed. Then the tiny measuring-worm decided to give it a try. Little by little, he inched up the mountain until at last he reached the summit. He found the boys, and led them on a great slide down the snowy slopes back to their tribe.

LENNI LENAPE see *DELAWARE*.

LITTLE PEOPLE are most commonly dwarfish beings who inhabit places outside camps and settlements and tend to cause mischief.

OJIBWAY travellers may see little people (the Maymaygwaysiwuk) paddling their stone canoes or playing along large cliffs. They live in the rocks and come and go through cracks and crevices, and one must always be on guard for them. The *WYANDOT* say they are old enough to remember the Flood, and the *PASSAMAQUODDY* believe they were here before *GLUSKAP*. In a *MICMAC* tale, the little people (Pukalutumush) are identified as the creators of petroglyphs.

The Tewa *PUEBLO* envisage their *TWIN* war gods, who were monster-slayers, as Towa É, which translates as "little people".

LODGE is a general term used to describe a permanent native dwelling. In the Great Plains, the earthlodge is a dome-shaped structure with a log frame. It is covered with earth or sods, and its floors are dug below ground level. The term may also be used to refer to other similar dwellings, such as tepees, which are covered with bark, skins or woven mats, and certain ceremonial structures.

L

THE DARK SIDE

ONSTERS EXIST in mythology to give shape and meaning to the unknown, the dangerous and the unwanted. Many story-tellers describe how, when the earth was still young, terrible creatures raged across the land, threatening the fragile harmony of human and animal beings in the new world. By the act of destroying these monsters, supernatural beings created the heroic, defined the limits of good and evil, and established supernatural power as an overwhelming force. But, while cosmic beasts disappeared, other dangerous creatures retreated only to the margins of the world, lurking just beyond familiar horizons, in the darkness or deep under water. Some of these are fearsome apparitions and the stuff of nightmare: bodiless heads or hideously deformed animals. Others,

including many of the "little people" that travellers encounter, cause accidents and other irritations in daily life. Still others, such as the great horned serpents who live under lakes and rivers in Algonquian territory, have the capacity for positive as well as negative acts. This acknowledgement of life's dark side resolves the fundamental contradiction of nature – that it is at one time both a nurturing and a destructive force.

A THUNDERBIRD sits atop a modern Kwakiutl totem pole. The association of thunder and lightning with giant birds may come from the way a thunderstorm soars across the sky, spreading dark squall lines across the horizon under a dark central mass, pierced by flashing light.

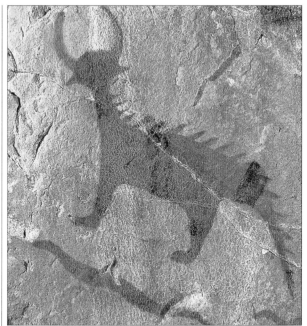

MISHIPIZHEU (left), the great horned serpent, is painted in red ochre on a sheer granite cliff overlooking Agawa Bay, Lake Superior. Travellers appeased this powerful manitou with prayers and offerings so that he would keep the waters calm as they passed.

A PLUMED SERPENT (below left) rises from the desert rocks of the Galisteo Basin, south of Santa Fe, New Mexico. Tewa people inhabited this region from the late 13th century until the Pueblo Revolt in 1680. Their abundant rock art still speaks of the powerful spiritual forces in the desert landscape.

THE IMAGE (below) of a mountain lion is etched into a slab of sandstone in northeastern Arizona's Painted Desert by an unknown prehistoric artist. The most dangerous forces in the spiritual world usually took the form of the most dangerous animals in real life.

PALRAIUK (below) the sea monster, gorged with the partly dismembered remains of one unfortunate victim, chases a kayak, seeking more prey. This Yupik walrus ivory engraving expresses the wariness of the Inuit whale hunter in the unpredictable Arctic seas.

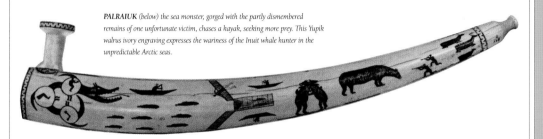

53

M

LODGE BOY AND THROWN AWAY are the main characters in the *HIDATSA* version of a story cycle about heroic *TWINS* that is told throughout the Plains.

The cycle begins with a pregnant woman inviting a stranger into her *LODGE* while her husband is away. In some versions the stranger is Double Face, a monster with eyes, nose and mouth on the back of his head. The woman offers to serve food to her guest, and he convinces her that he must have it served on her abdomen. When she complies, he cuts through the meat into her body, killing her and delivering her twin sons. He throws one in a spring and keeps one in the lodge. When the woman's husband returns, the monster flees, leaving one child and the body of the wife behind. The man buries his wife and raises Lodge Boy. The other child, Thrown Away, only comes in to eat while the father is away. At last, the man captures Thrown Away, and takes the wildness out of him by burning incense in his nose. The twins then go about slaying monsters, including Double Face. In a *WICHITA* version, the father goes to live in the sky, and the twins follow when their work is done. The *SARCEE*, *BLACK-FOOT*, *GROS VENTRE* and *ARAPAHO* join this story with another on the life of *DIRTY BOY*.

LONE MAN (*MANDAN*) was the companion of First Creator, who was responsible for the beginning of the cosmos. The two creators made the earth from mud brought from the primeval sea by Duck, and populated it with all living things. Lone Man's later exploits included the release of buffalo from the control of Speckled *EAGLE*, the rescue of the Mandan from a world flood by building a watertight stockade around the village, and the imprisonment, in a tomb of black rock, of the monster-slayer Foolish Doer, who was too frightening to remain in the company of human beings.

IN A COMING OF AGE ceremony in a Mandan earthlodge village, the young initiates, dragging bison skulls attached to their flesh, are each supported by two dancers as they run around a sacred "ark". This was the end of the Okipa, a four-day religious ceremony that renewed tribal spirit and ensured a plentiful supply of buffalo for the year. (PAINTING BY GEORGE CATLIN, 1832.)

When his work was done, Lone Man left for the south, whence he communicates as the south wind.

LOON WOMAN, according to a myth among peoples of northern California, attempted to commit incest and, in so doing, caused a world fire. One day, she saw a long hair floating on the water (or found it in a comb) and was enthralled by it. In order to discover its owner, she compared it to the hair of her ten brothers and, finding that it was from the eldest brother's head, fell hopelessly in love with him. She secretly lay with him while camping and he, horrified, freed himself and put a rotten log in his place. To escape the horror of her act, he ran home and ordered his family to jump into a basket that would carry them into the sky. But the sister awoke, saw the rising basket and set fire to the family's lodge. Unfortunately, while the basket was still rising, *COYOTE*, who had happened by, peered over the edge; the basket fell and the family perished in the flames. The sister gathered up the victims' blackened hearts and wore them as a necklace – seen as the black neck-band of the common loon (great northern diver).

LOST-ACROSS-THE-OCEAN is a *CULTURE HERO* of the *YUROK*, *HUPA*, *KARUK* and *WIYOT* of north-western California.

The Hupa say he sprang from earth, released deer and salmon, instituted childbirth, created landscape features and instituted the Jumping Dance to counteract disease. After killing cannibals and transforming cannibal soap-roots into food, he created tribes by defecation. When his work was done, he crossed the ocean, and lives beyond the end of the sky.

THE LUISEÑO people are an Uto-Aztecan-speaking tribe that once occupied a large area of coastal southern California within the San Luis Rey and Santa Margarita River basins. They lived on the abundant marine life of the warm Pacific coastal waters and harvested acorns from the oak-covered coastal hills. In 1891, the Act for the Relief of the Mission Indians established five Luiseño reservations, some of which included traditional farmland. Today, the people living near the rivers run successful orchard operations, and have market gardens and domesticated animals. Those in the drier inlands, where water is very often scarce, are limited by their surroundings to relying on subsistence farming.

MAHTIGWESS see *HARES*.

THE MAIDU [Northeast, Northwest, Valley], speakers of Penutian languages, live in the northeastern interior of California. The Northeast Maidu, Northwest Maidu (once known as the Digger), and Valley Maidu all speak separate languages. They are fishers, hunters and gatherers who share cultural traits with the more northerly Northwest Coast peoples, as well as with adjacent Plateau and Great Basin groups. Although they were dispersed before the 20th century, they now have a small land base within their traditional territory.

THE MAKAH live on the Olympic Peninsula, south of Vancouver Island. They are the most southerly of the Wakashan-speakers, and so are related to the *NOOTKA* and *KWAKIUTL*. Like other Northwest Coast peoples, they hunted, fished and gathered in the midst of abundant natural resources. The Makah were highly skilled hunters of sea mammals, pursuing whales and fur seals in the open sea. The Treaty of Neah Bay established the Makah Reservation in 1855. One of their original village settlements, at Ozette, near the northwestern tip of the Olympic Peninsula, was partly buried in a mudslide some 500 years ago and rediscovered in the 1960s. The mud had preserved the remains of the cedar-plank houses in the village, and all the tools and other material goods used in the course of daily life.

THE MALISEET (Malecite) are an Algonquian people who hunted, fished and gathered along the rivers of southern New Brunswick and adjoining parts of northern Maine. The seasonal rhythm took them

such as the *SIOUX* "wakan" and the *IROQUOIS* "orenda".

MASAWU (*HOPI*) is the *KACHINA* who greeted the first people as they emerged from the underworld. The kachina dancer charged with impersonating this god does so by wearing a skeleton mask with enormous white eye sockets.

MASTAMHO
see *BROTHER GODS*.

THE MASTER/MISTRESS OF ANIMALS is a god or spirit who controls animals (see also *MOTHER OF ANIMALS*). This being may be a central figure in the culture's belief system (such as Sedna, the *SEA MOTHER* of the *INUIT*) or a malicious spirit who captures either all the animals or a crucial game animal species, thus causing the people to starve until a hero sets the animals free.

In an *UTE* scenario, all the animal people were short of food except for the Crows, who always seemed to have plenty to eat. No one knew where the buffalo had gone, but the Crows had a vast tent that they would not let anyone else look into. As soon as someone peeped in, *CROW* would poke something in their eye. Finally, Darning Needle went to look; he was so slim that, when Crow poked something through the peephole, it went right by, and Darning Needle discovered Crow's secret: he had captured all the buffalo. The animals had a council and made a plan for releasing them. Weasel transformed himself into a dog and remained in the area, while the rest of the people broke camp and left; the Crow children found the dog and took it back to their camp. When the Crows were asleep, Weasel let all the buffalo out.

As the plenitude of animals depends on the will of gods or heroes, people ever after must pay due respect to the animal spirits in order to be sure of a continuing

THIS MEDICINE BUNDLE and small whistle was worn by a warrior of a Great Plains tribe around his neck to give him spiritual power.

supply of food. This is why hunters set aside time before, during and after the hunt to ensure that the proper rituals, prayers and procedures are carried out, as the *CREE* do in their *BEAR RITUALS*.

MASTSHINGKE
see under *HARES*.

MATAVILYA see *BROTHER GODS*.

MEDICINE is a translation of various concepts related to spiritual efficacy. Medicine is invested in an object or substance used in curing or in some other beneficial way. Native people do not attribute its power to its pharmaceutical properties – it may have none – but to its capacity to harness and direct spiritual forces. Hence, a herb or other substance, or a sacred smoking *PIPE* or other object, may provide, or be, good medicine.

from interior to coast, giving them access to a great diversity of food resources, including moose, deer and beaver, fish and waterfowl, clams and other shellfish, and seals and porpoises. During the 18th century, they joined the *WABANAKI* confederacy. They now occupy reservations in New Brunswick, Maine and Quebec.

MANABUSH, MANABOZHO
see *NANABUSH*.

THE MANDAN are a Siouan people who lived along the Missouri River, near its confluence with the Knife River in North Dakota, in large villages of earthlodges (see *LODGE*). They raised squash, corn (maize), sunflowers and tobacco along the fertile and moist flood plains of the river and its tributaries. They also hunted buffalo, which provided them with essen-

MÁTO-TÓPE, or Four Bears (c. 1795–1837), was a highly respected military and religious leader among the Mandan. He was given his name after a skirmish with the Assiniboine, in which he fought with especially great ferocity.

tial meat and hides for clothing. Along with their traditional allies, the *HIDATSA* and the *ARIKARA*, the Mandan share the Fort Berthold Reservation in North Dakota.

MANITOU is an Algonquian term, used primarily by the *OJIBWAY* to describe the most powerful supernatural beings, as well as the all-pervasive spiritual essence they symbolize. This personification, from the great spirit Gitchi-Manitou (or Kitchi-, or Chi-) to the numerous spirit-beings who dwell in the Ojibway landscape, sets it apart from the other Native American concepts of immanent power,

THE MILKY WAY is an important astronomical configuration for a number of different tribes. Many believe it is the pathway to another world.

THE MENOMINEE people are an Algonquian tribe who lived in the forests between Lake Michigan and Lake Superior, where they hunted deer, bear and other forest game, fished the lakes and rivers, and gathered wild rice, roots, berries and other plant foods. Their name means "wild rice people". The tribe once occupied over 3.6 million ha (9 million acres) of land in present-day central and mideastern Wisconsin and part of the Upper Peninsula of Michigan. Their reservation was established in 1854, leaving the tribe with only 94,700 ha (234,000 acres) of land.

MESQUAKI see *FOX*.

THE MICMAC (Mi'kmaq) are a hardy seagoing people who originally occupied most of present-day Nova Scotia, northern New Brunswick, part of northern Maine, and southern Newfoundland. They were among the first tribes to be contacted by Europeans and their missionaries, at the beginning of the 17th century. During the 18th century, they joined the *WABANAKI* confederacy. They pursued the nomadic hunting, fishing and gathering life typical of maritime Algonquian tribes, moving in a seasonal round between the interior, where they hunted moose, deer and other small game, and the coast, where they paddled their ocean-going canoes in the open waters of the Atlantic in pursuit of whales and porpoises. The tribe has a number of small reservations in Nova Scotia, New Brunswick, Maine, Quebec and Newfoundland. (See also *THE STRANGERS, NEW GODS*)

THE MIDÉWIWIN, or Grand *MEDICINE* Society, was an organization of *SHAMANS* devoted to curing disease. It flourished among the *OJIBWAY* and other Great Lakes Algonquians during the 19th and early 20th centuries. It was a *SECRET SOCIETY*, open to men and women, who worked their way through a number of degrees (levels of attainment), which incorporated beliefs, rituals and curing techniques of increasing complexity. Midé shamans engraved or painted birch-bark scrolls with pictographic records of their origin myths, ceremonies and songs. There are still adherents to the Midéwiwin philosophy practising today, though the organization is no longer central to the religious activities of the people.

THE MILKY WAY, the white arch of stars that dominates the moonless night sky, has inspired many theories about its origin.

The Mescalero *APACHE*, who call it the Scattered Stars, believe that one of the *TWIN* War Gods dropped a container of seeds during a fight with his brother, and the seeds scattered across the sky. Many peoples believe that the Milky Way is a pathway to a sky world or to the land of the dead. The *SEMINOLE* explain that their creator, Breath-maker, blew into the sky, and the vapour from his breath made a pathway leading to the City of the West. This is where the good souls go, carried there by the Big Dipper. (See also *THE LIVING SKY*)

MINK, a rather disreputable *TRICKSTER* popular in Northwest Coast narratives, is a useful foil for *RAVEN*. He is generally involved in sordid intrigues with women, most of which end in disaster.

MISHIPIZHEU (*OJIBWAY*), a horned serpent, lives under lakes and rivers. Mishipizheu (literally, "Great Lynx") is a very important spiritual presence in Ojibway culture. Unlike many other monsters, his status is closer to that of a god, for he exercises power over the vast network of lakes and rivers within Ojibway lands in the Canadian Shield (north of the Great Lakes).

In some accounts, he was responsible for the primordial flood. He occupies caverns and tunnels beneath the lakes, so he is able to travel easily anywhere in the region. He is said to stir up the waters of lakes and turn rivers into dangerous rapids to drown people – it is therefore wise to leave a bit of tobacco or some other small offering when one enters a lake that might be one of Mishipizheu's many lairs. When he travels on the land, he crawls like a giant leech, saturating the ground and leaving swamps and quicksand behind.

The Ojibway of the Lake Temagami region of northern Ontario describe him as the source of all snakes. When he was crossing a lake, a bolt of lightning shattered him, and all the pieces turned into small snakes: the ancestors of all the snakes of today.

He may also provide *MEDICINE*, but is so dangerous that his power can even overwhelm *SHAMANS*. In one incident, a shaman dreamed that if he struck the water with a stick and sang a special song the spirits would reward him. He did so, but, as he struck the water, it erupted into a violent whirlpool, and the great serpent rose up to confront him. The man boldly (and greedily) asked the creature for medicine to make him healthy, rich and prosperous. Mishipizheu lowered his head, and the shaman saw a bright red substance similar to red ochre (or copper – Mishipizheu was the guardian of native copper mines on the shores of Lake Superior) between his horns. The man scraped this medicine into a piece of birch bark, and the serpent told him how to use it. For a time, the medicine worked, and the man prospered, but in fact he paid a terrible price – eventually his wife and children died, and he lived out his wretched life poor and alone. (See also *THE DARK SIDE*)

THE MIWOK (Me-wuk) [Coastal, Lake, Valley] are a Penutian-speaking people who lived in three distinctive ecological zones in central California. The Coastal Miwok settled on the central California coast, while the Lake and Valley Miwok (including the Sierra Miwok, who live in the mountains to the east) occupied the interior. They had a sophisticated preservation technology, storing the masses of acorns they gathered in granaries of woven branches and grass, suspended above the ground. The coastal people had the most diverse food supply, as they had access to shellfish and other sea creatures, in addition to the freshwater fish, deer, other small game, acorns and other plant foods along the lakes and rivers. They were heavily affected by European contact from the 16th century onwards – in 1578 they encountered the English explorer, Sir Francis Drake.

Over the centuries, the Miwok suffered disease, missionizing and, after the discovery of gold in the region in 1848, death at the hands of prospectors and settlers. They resisted for a short time, but their rebellion was crushed in 1851, and they were forcibly removed to several *rancherias* (small reservations) in their traditional territory.

MOAPA see under *PAIUTE*.

THE MODOC, speakers of a Penutian language, once occupied the rugged mountains of the Cascade Range along the Oregon–California border, where they fished the rivers for salmon, gathered roots in the drier uplands, and hunted small game. The regionally important sacred site, Mt Shasta, was once part of their homeland.

The Modoc lost their lands as a result of the Council Grove Treaty of 1864, and were removed to the Klamath Reservation in Oregon, which they shared with the Klamath (a closely related and culturally similar tribe) and the *PAIUTE*. In the late 1860s, discontent with their treatment by the Klamath provoked a group of Modoc under Kintpuash (known as Captain Jack) to leave the reservation and return to their homeland. The United States military crushed the renegades in 1872–3. They executed Kintpuash and three of his followers, and exiled the rest to the Quapaw Agency in Indian Territory (the Quapaw being an unrelated tribe who once lived in the area of present-day Arkansas). Soon after the

execution, grave robbers disinterred Kintpuash's body and displayed the remains in a carnival in the eastern states. The two Modoc groups, based in Oregon and Oklahoma, are now politically and culturally separate.

MOHAWK see *IROQUOIS*.

THE MOJAVE (Mohave), speakers of a Yuman language, live along the Colorado River and in the Colorado basin in Arizona and California. They grow corn (maize) and beans on river flood plains, net fish and gather mesquite and other plant foods. Unlike most other aboriginal groups, the Mojave continue to occupy part of their traditional homelands – largely because their semi-desert environ-

A MOJAVE female doll is decorated with face paint and wears trade bead earrings and necklaces.

ment had little economic value for the incoming white people, but also because the tribe resisted relocation to reservations.

MOMOY (*CHUMASH*) is a grandmother who gives help to child monster-slayers. The word is the same as that for the hallucinogenic drug, toloache, made from datura, or jimsonweed. In one account relating to the use of the drug in a tribal rite, the grandmother washed her hands in a bowl of water and gave it to her grandson to drink so that he could become braver.

MONDAMIN (Southern *OJIBWAY*) is the male corn spirit, who generates corn from his body.

THE MONTAGNAIS [Innu], an Algonquian hunting and gathering people, live in the vast boreal forests of central Quebec, where they range in small bands, following the seasonal patterns of moose, deer and other game, fish, wildfowl and wild plants. They were heavily involved in the French fur trade,

THE MOON is portrayed on this wooden mask which is carved in the typical Tsimshian style of smooth, restrained facial modelling, with subdued colours and a lifelike finish.

beginning in the 17th century, and hence were one of the first tribes to be described by Europeans. While the fur-trade economy forever altered the tribe's way of life, their remoteness has helped them to retain much of their traditional culture. They are now joined with the *NASKAPI* and collectively known as the Innu.

MONTEZUMA see *POSAYAMO*.

THE MOON, with its prominence in the sky, its predictable phases and its relationship with the sun, has inspired a wide variety of mythical interpretations.

To the Coast *SALISH*, Moon is a *TRANSFORMER*, born of the union of a woman and a star, who gave the people salmon, and other fish and game (see *STAR HUSBAND*). To the *MAIDU*, he is a rather villainous *TRICKSTER* who steals children.

THE TRICKSTER

THE CREATIVE BEINGS responsible for the complex texture of North American cultures established methods for living that enabled people to thrive over thousands of years. Yet humans must always face the tension between appropriate and inappropriate thoughts and actions, reflecting the vagaries of a natural world that both sustains life and takes it. Mirroring this reality, transformers and culture heroes were quixotically human, with the same lusts, desires and foibles as the people they would create. Raven brought daylight to the Tsimshian, for example, by tricking an old chief who kept it in a box on the Nass River. Raven became a spruce needle, entered the chief's daughter in a drink of water, impregnated her, was born,

and then, as a small child, took the box at an unguarded moment, quickly changing back to his original self and flying off with his prize. This was no altruistic act: he released the daylight in anger, after some fishing people refused him a feed of *oolichan* (a smelt-like fish, very high in fat). By giving the tricksters human capacities and imperfections, and by treating creation as the incidental acts of great beings pursuing their own agendas, the story-tellers wisely create realistic parallels between life as it is lived and its origins.

THE SPIDER-LIKE TRICKSTER *Iktomi is part of the essence of the Siouan world, at once graceful like the sweep of birds though the sky and jagged as a leafless tree, a singer of songs and a crafty predator. (PAINTING BY OGLALA LAKOTA ARTIST ARTHUR AMIOTTE.)*

THE WOLVERINE (left), the largest member of the weasel family, is a ferocious scavenger that feeds mainly off dead animals. It can quickly devastate the food caches crucial to the survival of the northern forest peoples. To fit its reputation as a glutton, it may also attack and kill other mammals and even caribou – especially if such animals are injured or weakened by winter hunger.

RAVEN (above) releases the sun from its box. The raven is a worthy trickster – black, portly and strutting, with large beak and bright, black eyes. In settlements, he is a crafty thief, like his cousin the crow, and he rules his patch of forest aggressively, watching for intruders from high in a tree. (SILK-SCREEN PRINT BY THE KWAKIUTL ARTIST CALVIN HUNT.)

THE COYOTE (left), grey and short-haired, is a creature ever-watchful on the boundaries of humankind, loping along a beach or skulking at the edge of a field by day, a ghostly shadow at dusk, and an eerie howl in the night.

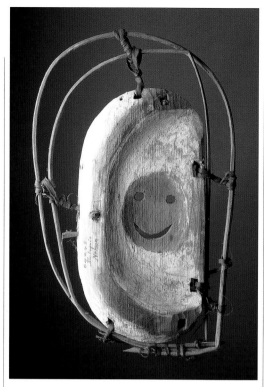

shaman towards the hole in the sky that connects the earth to the moon. If Alinnaq gets the water, he drops whale effigies made of lamp tar into the pots, and these become powerful hunting amulets.

MOON WIFE (*ALEUT*) is a character used to explain the different phases of the moon.

Two young women, fascinated by the moon, spent their nights making symbolic love to him by basking in his light in the shelter of a skin boat. Then one night he appeared to them as a young man. He told them that he would take the most patient of the two into the sky to be his wife – patience being necessary because the work in the sky was hard. As the three rose into the sky, one could not resist looking down, and she fell back to the boat. The other, who went to live in Moon's house (a *barrabara*, a timbered, earth-banked pit house), was frustrated and lonely. Her husband usually slept during the day and worked all night, but she could never be sure when he would come home, and he always refused her request to accompany him during his nightly tasks.

One night he permitted her to leave home so that she could amuse herself, but he warned her not to go into two particular *barrabara*, for each had a curtain under which she must never look. Predictably, she could not resist going into these forbidden places. In the first one, she raised the curtain and saw a half-moon, quarter-moon and a sliver of moon; in the second, she found a full moon, one almost full, and one more than half full. They were like masks, and when she tried to put one over her face, it stuck – so she could not hide her transgression from her husband. As the secret was out, he decided to let her help him. He would do his rounds with the full moon, and then she would take over, wearing the different phases, while he rested.

THE MOTHER OF ANIMALS

gives birth to game or produces it from her body. Many cultures in the Arctic and Subarctic refer to animal mothers in their mythologies – examples of the universal mythological theme of the *MASTER/ MISTRESS OF ANIMALS*.

The Kodiak Island *ALEUT* believe that a single young woman gave birth to all animals, one after another. The *HARE* tribe relate the story of Egg Woman who, after being abused by human males, became mother of the hares. In a *TAHLTAN* narrative, a pregnant woman, abandoned, gave birth to moose, caribou and other animals, thus becoming Atsentmá (meat mother). Sedna, the *SEA MOTHER* of the *INUIT*, begins as an unwanted woman. A man (commonly her father) throws her out of his boat and then chops off her fingers as she clings to the

MOON MAN (Alinnaq) (*INUIT*) interprets the close relationship of sun and moon as a dramatic tale of forbidden love and eternal longing.

A man, Alinnaq, secretly lusted after his sister. One night he slipped into her bed and had sex with her, and she, discovering the identity of the lover, cut off her breast, demanded that he eat it, and fled into the darkness with a torch of lamp moss. The brother followed with another torch, but he fell in the snow and the light was almost extinguished. They both rose into the sky, the sister becoming the sun and her brother the moon. He pursues her still and, when there is an eclipse, they say that he has caught her.

Alinnaq is the major deity in the western Arctic, among the Tikigaq and other Alaskan Iñupiat. He controls the game (replacing Sedna, the *MISTRESS OF ANIMALS* in the central and eastern Arctic), keeping a vast tub of whales and seals, and running herds of caribou around

the inner walls of his igloo. *SHAMANS* confront Alinnaq in person when food is scarce. The most important ritual takes place during the spring, when whale hunters seek Alinnaq's help. During the climax of the ceremony, the women stand on their igloos as the moon rises, shout at the moon and raise pots of water blessed by the

MOTHER CORN and other earth deities were revered by the Navajo. This 19th-century rug depicts yei figures, earth spirits associated with the fertility of corn. Such images are properly made as sand paintings, but they are too sacred to be exposed to public view. Hence, Navajo artists translate the sand painting motifs into weavings and paintings.

MUDHEADS, or koshares, are depicted tumbling madly down a ladder, upsetting the sober tone of a Hopi religious ceremony. Their general silliness opens the audience to important moral lessons, as they inevitably pay for their impudence. (THE DELIGHT MAKERS, PAINTING BY FRED KABOTIE.)

gunwale. The fingers change into seals and walruses, and she sinks to the bottom and becomes the ruler of the animals of the sea. There she awaits the attention of *SHAMANS* seeking a plentiful food supply.

MOTHER CORN is the personification of the important corn (maize) plant as a goddess.

NISHANÚ NATCHITAK first made giants, but he eventually killed them because they mocked him. He planted some as corn kernels and drowned the rest in a world flood. He also planted corn in the sky; when it matured, he took an ear and turned it into Mother Corn, who came down from the sky world to lead the new people (the *ARIKARA*) up out of the ground. A badger and a mole helped Mother Corn by burrowing upward through the earth. When they emerged, she led them westward past three obstacles (a chasm, a thick forest and a lake) and then departed for the sky. The people lacked order, however, and ended up fighting and killing one another, so Nishánu sent Mother Corn back with a man to be their leader. While she taught the people the proper rituals, the new leader showed them how to make war.

MOTHER EARTH and **FATHER SKY** (*NAVAJO*) are two cosmic beings, stretched out like a man lying on top of a woman. The space between them has several layers (air and then stars), and the stars are either attached to the sky or are hanging down from it. The concept of a Mother Earth and Father Sky, once absent from the oral traditions of many cultures, is now an integral part of modern pan-Indian religions.

MUDHEADS (*PUEBLO*) are sacred clowns. During mainly solemn ceremonials, the mudheads break the tension with ridiculous antics and silly pantomimes. They are not trivial characters, but rather holy people who play an integral role in the sacred rites.

In one *ZUNI* characterization, the Mudheads are not very bright, so a man tries to teach them a few simple tasks. When they try to climb a ladder, they get all tangled up. When they try to work out how

A YUPIK SEALSKIN MASK possibly used in a Bladder Festival (Nakaquik) to show respect to seals so that they would continue to let hunters kill them. The Yupik traditionally destroyed their dance masks after use – returning them to nature.

to sit on a chair, they attempt every way but the right way: one sits on top and tumbles off, another sits underneath, another backwards and another upside down. When they try to build a house, they start with the roof and then have to try to build downwards with several Mudheads holding it up. Then they build one from the inside, but it has no doors or windows, so they become trapped.

MUSP AND KOMOL (*CHINOOK*) are *TRANSFORMER TWINS* whose origin is explained in a variation of the *BEAR MOTHER* story.

A young woman abducted by a grizzly *BEAR* gave birth to a son and a daughter. Her brothers rescued her, and she eventually married a village chief. Unfortunately, since she happened to be a laughing monster and a devouring monster, she accidentally swallowed the whole village. When she coughed up her husband, he had lost his legs, so she hung him on the wall in a basket. Incredibly, she managed to conceive with him and bore two sons, the heroes. They seized their terrifying mother, shook her bones out of her skin and turned these into a dog, their faithful companion. After teaching people how to catch salmon, dig shellfish and hunt whales, the *TWINS* turned into boulders that are still visible today.

NAKAQUIK (*INUIT*), the Bladder Festival, is a winter solstice ceremony in which the bladders of animals killed during the year are ritually returned to the sea (and to Sedna) to ensure abundant game.

NAKOTA see *SIOUX*.

NANABUSH is the principal CULTURE HERO and TRANSFORMER of the OJIBWAY. He is known by several different names, including Manabush, Manabozho, Nanabozho, Wenebojo and Winabojo. This is the result of dialect variation across Ojibway culture. The MENOMINEE, close relatives of the Ojibway, call him Menapus, or "Big Rabbit" (see HARES). He shares many attributes and story types with the hero of Algonquian tribes south of the Great Lakes, known as WISAKEDJAK or Wisaka, and the hero of north-eastern coastal Algonquians, GLUSKAP. He also appears in the WALAM OLUM of the DELAWARE peoples.

Nanabush is a highly complex figure, combining the attributes of culture hero, transformer and TRICKSTER. He gave the northern landscape its character and created many living things, fought evil MANITOUS and brought to the Ojibway the defining elements of their culture. In a MIDÉWIWIN society story of CREATION, Nanabush made men from earth, but they disappeared – stolen by evil manitous – until he created Thunderers to watch over them. In a Wisconsin Chippewa (southern Ojibway) account, in which he is called Wenebojo, he came into this world from blood clots that a cold and starving old woman picked from the carcass of a moose and stored in a mitten. As soon as he emerged, he transformed himself into a small rabbit, crossed a great ocean and stole fire from the people living there for his grandmother.

Some of his transformations combine ribald antics and, perhaps, some rather darker sexual undertones. He once turned himself into a caribou, feigned death and allowed all the birds and animals to consume him until only his anus was left. When a turkey buzzard flew down to eat this and, in so doing, stuck its head up the anus, Wenebojo tightened his rectum and captured the bird. The

buzzard escaped when Wenebojo joined a game of lacrosse – but it scraped its head pulling it out, which is why this bird is red and scabby and smells bad.

For all his antics and noble acts, Wenebojo was subject to lust, envy, greed and the other foibles of humankind – and generally suffered for his temptations. In another southern Ojibway story that carries a serious lesson about incest, Wenebojo tricked his daughters into marrying him, and eventually felt so ashamed that he crawled into the open mouth of a muskie (a species of predatory fish) and remains there to this day.

NANIH WAIYA (CHOCTAW) is a hill in Winston County, Mississippi, near the headwaters of the Pearl River. This is the place where the Choctaw and several related tribes emerged from the underworld. The first to emerge were the Muskogees (CREEKS), who then travelled east; next came the CHEROKEES, who moved to the north; then, the Chickasaws, who followed the Cherokee trail and settled near them in the north; and finally, the Choctaws, who stayed on the lands around Nanih Waiya.

NAVAJO WOMEN are preparing wool and weaving a carpet. The Navajo learned how to weave with native grasses and cotton from the Pueblos. In the 17th century, they obtained Spanish Churro sheep and began to work with wool, making fine blankets with simple but striking geometric designs. They began to make carpets during the late 19th century.

Some believe that Grasshopper Mother, who led the people through the shaft to the top of the hill, was killed when she stayed behind. To avenge her death, Aba, the creator, closed the entrance and transformed the murderers into ants. Others believe that the shaft remains open.

THE NASKAPI [Innu] live in the boreal forests of northern Quebec and Labrador. They follow the typical northern Algonquian cultural pattern, travelling through their lands in small bands, hunting caribou, moose, deer, bear, beaver and

THIS HIDE COAT is in the typical Naskapi decorative style, which consists of intricately painted linear and curvilinear geometric patterns. Such patterns were part of the Naskapi religious iconography. They first appeared on clothing during the early 18th century.

other large and small game, taking fish and waterfowl from the innumerable lakes and rivers, and gathering seasonally available food resources. Like the CREE and their other Algonquian neighbours, they especially prize the BEAR and conduct BEAR RITUALS to ensure success in the hunt and the propitiation of the species. They are now joined with their MONTAGNAIS neighbours to the south, and are known as the Innu.

THE NAVAJO [Dine] are an Athapascan-speaking people who gradually migrated south from the Athapascan homeland in the north-western Subarctic, and arrived in the Southwest about 1,000 years ago. When they arrived in this land of semi-arid mountains and plains,

O

they pursued their traditional hunting and gathering, but learned from the neighbouring PUEBLO tribes how to plant corn (maize). Early Spanish accounts record fields of corn surrounding Navajo settlements. This reliable food supply dramatically changed their lifestyle and became the focus of their religious beliefs, as it provided a powerful metaphor for the course of human life. Their economy changed again when they obtained sheep, goats and horses, and herding became their primary activity. They were aggressive, asserting their hold over a large territory impinging on the traditional homelands of the HOPI and other Pueblos. They drew much from these tribes, including weaving, sand painting, and aspects of religious belief. The Navajo Reservation is the largest in the US (more than 7.29 million ha/18 million acres).

NAYENEZGANI AND TOBADJISHTCHINI (NAVAJO), equating to the APACHE Monster-Slayer and CHILD-OF-THE-WATER, are the Navajo versions of the TWIN war gods conceived by CHANGING WOMAN after she exposed her body to the sun and dripping water.

NEZ PERCE, a Penutian-speaking tribe, had their homeland on the Columbia Plateau, in present-day Idaho, Washington and Oregon, where they hunted, fished and gathered along forested rivers. After they obtained horses, however, they began to live off the great buffalo herds that ranged throughout the northwestern Great Plains.

In 1855, the US government forced them to cede several million acres of territory. In 1863, the tribe lost most of its remaining 3.24 million ha (8 million acres) when they were forced into signing another treaty. This led to a war in 1877, during which Chief Joseph and some of his people tried to flee to Canada. The US military captured them just short of the border, after

a trek of 2,735 km (1,700 miles), and the chief never saw his homeland again. The poignant figure of Chief Joseph in surrender came to represent one of the most powerful symbols of the terrible, shameful destruction of the American Indian people. Today, the Nez Perce own or control 37,510 ha (92,685 acres) in north-central Idaho.

NISHANÚ NATCHITAK (Nesaru, Chief-Above) (ARIKARA) was the creator of human beings. He first made giants, who proved too unruly and disrespectful. After saving a few smaller people by transforming them into grains of corn (maize) and storing them in a cave, he caused a flood to rid the world of the giants. He then planted corn in the heavens and transformed an ear of this corn into a woman, MOTHER CORN. She eventually led the people out of the underworld and gave them their culture.

THE NOOTKA [Nuu-Chah-Nulth] is a Wakashan-speaking tribe that occupied the western and southwestern shores of Vancouver

CHIEF JOSEPH was the tragic, heroic resistance leader of the Nez Perce. To avoid incarceration at the Fort Lapwai, Idaho, reservation in 1877, he fled north with a small band of followers, seeking freedom. The US Cavalry cornered the demoralized remnants of his band just 64 km (40 miles) from sanctuary in Canada. Chief Joseph spent the rest of his life in exile.

THIS NOOTKA HAT is made of woven cedar bark and decorated with whales and other clan symbols. Only a chief with whaling privileges could wear it, as the symbols are both displays of chiefly power and representations of important clan ancestors.

Island. Like their Pacific Coast mainland relatives, they lived in coastal villages of large communal cedar-plank houses and harvested the abundant resources of the coastal waters and forests. Skilled hunters of sea mammals, they braved the open waters of the Pacific in large cedar canoes to pursue whales and seals. As a coastal people, they were contacted early by European explorers, including the Spanish explorer Juan de Fuca (1592) and the English explorers James Cook (1776–8) and George Vancouver (1792). While they suffered the depredations typically caused by European contact (disease, loss of traditional culture through missionary activity and trade, and loss of territory), their structured maritime society has allowed them to retain the essence of their cultural identity.

NORELPUTUS (WINTU) was a prophet who composed a new set of myths in the late 19th century. He created an elaborate mythology that revolved around the high

god Olelbis (One-Who-Is-Above) and his consort Mem Loimis (Water Woman).

NUSMATTA (BELLA COOLA) is a house in the sky that contains all the mythical narratives related by story-tellers.

OBSIDIAN (YUROK) personifies the black volcanic glass that was the best and most sought-after raw material for prehistoric stone tool-making.

A young man became obsessed with catching a fiery mass that he saw floating down a river. After failing several times, he fell into a deep depression and wept uncontrollably. Finally, after setting a net in the river and a snare on the bottom, he caught his elusive prey, a fish-like creature. He told it that he was lonely and had no one to talk to, and it told him that it kept moving down the river because it wanted to leave its home. The man had been kind and respectful, so the creature, Obsidian, told him that, from then on, it would be beautiful and valuable, and would endure as long as people continued to respect it through rituals. Obsidian revealed to the man where it grew up and then never spoke again. Thereafter, the people were always able to find obsidian for their tools.

DEATH & AFTERLIFE

DEATH IS NOT ABSOLUTE in a world where nothing is inanimate, and time does not retreat endlessly into extinction; people withdraw from bodily existence, just as the culture heroes did after the age of transformation. Those supernatural beings were responsible for the fact of death, usually because of some heroic failing. Among the Modoc, for example, a chief named Kumokums allowed people to go to the Land of the Dead because his village was overcrowded – unfortunately, he did not reckon on losing members of his own family. The path of the dead may lead into an underworld, into a remote land beyond the horizon, or into the sky. Most cultures hope that it will be a place of physical and spiritual ease: thus, some tribes in the rugged Northwest Coast interior speak of a welcoming refuge, a wonderful flat land of sweet-smelling flowers that they refer to as Prairie Town. The longing for the return of the dead to life is expressed in stories of living people who, Orpheus-like, journey to the land of the dead to retrieve a loved one. During the terrible suffering caused by the white invasion, this longing occupied entire tribes on the Great Plains; by dancing the Ghost Dance, they hoped to revive their ancestors and return the world to its original state.

THE STARS *were the souls of all the people who had died, in some tribal philosophies. This belief persists in accounts of the origin of specific constellations, such as the Pleiades, which are commonly held to be six or seven sisters, transported from the earth into the sky.*

DANCERS (above) on the Northwest Coast wear masks that display their clan status and heritage, and imbue them with the power of the clan ancestors they represent. The renewal of spiritual links through ceremony helps the tribe to maintain its cultural identity.

(PAINTING BY PAUL KANE, 19TH CENTURY.)

THIS TABLEAU (left) represents life and death among the Sioux residing near Fort Pierre, Dakota Territory (present-day South Dakota). The platform burial exposed the deceased to the life-giving elements and to the sky, allowing the spirit to rejoin the air from which it came.

(ENGRAVING, 1844, FROM A PAINTING BY KARL BODMER.)

OLD BEAR (above) was a Mandan shaman. The shaman's spiritual powers and knowledge of ceremony ensured that the dead received the respect necessary to release the soul back into the spirit world.

(PAINTING BY GEORGE CATLIN, 1832.)

TANANA INDIAN SPIRIT HOUSES (above) lie in a cemetery at Tok, southern Alaska. St Timothy's Episcopal Mission was established in 1912 on the north side of the Tanana River, several miles from the present-day community of Tok. Because of the influence of Christianity, the Tanana people blend traditional and Christian themes in their burials.

OFFERING SITES are places associated with supernatural beings and events, where supplicants wishing for some good fortune leave offerings. Offering rituals are a common part of worship at sacred places.

In an example from the Plateau region, a large, upright boulder, more than 2 m (6 feet) tall and roughly in the shape of a human body, used to stand in the homeland of the Kalispel tribe, near the present border with Canada (it was eventually destroyed by settlers or by construction activity).

To the OKANAGAN and COLVILLE peoples, this rock was Camas Woman, or Wishing Stone – the name is associated with camas root (Camassia esculenta), a powerful MEDICINE. A woman named Blue Flower journeyed to the Okanagan valley in search of a young man she hoped to marry, the eldest of three brothers. She carried a basket filled with camas bulbs. When she met the brothers, the two younger ones started fighting over her, just as COYOTE happened by. He began to laugh at the spectacle, which annoyed Blue Flower so much that she spoke sharply to him. Insulted, Coyote turned the lower part of her body into stone, transformed the three young men into three mountains, and abandoned her. When he happened to come back that way again, he discovered that she had thrown the camas bulbs back to her home in the Kalispel region – she did not want camas to grow in the Okanagan valley – and used her own power to transform herself completely into stone. Impressed by her strength and perseverance, Coyote gave her special power as a wishing stone.

In another Okanagan version, probably influenced by Roman Catholic teachings, the name came during a time of great sickness, when the Great Chief Above instructed a SHAMAN to gather all the people at the Wishing Stone. When the sun reached its height, a

bright light appeared and a beautiful woman floated down. She gave the people camas bulbs, with instructions on planting them, and told them that in the spring the blue flowers would be so thick they would look like a lake. They were to gather the roots in the autumn, use them as medicine, and they would never again have the sickness. Suddenly, a breeze lifted her into the sky, and she disappeared into the clouds. From that time on, the people left gifts for her at the Wishing Stone.

THE OJIBWAY (Anishinabe) [Northern, Plains, Southern], who now prefer their traditional name Anishinabe, are a large Algonquian tribe that once controlled a vast, rugged territory around the shores of Lake Superior.

They may be generally divided into three groups: the Northern Ojibway (including the Salteaux), who occupy the boreal forests north of the upper Great Lakes; the Plains Ojibway, who live at the edge of the eastern Great Plains; and the Southern Ojibway (commonly called the Chippewa), who lived in the mixed deciduous and coniferous forests and prairies south of the upper Great Lakes. Each group adapted to its surroundings. The northern Ojibway were hunters and gatherers similar to the CREE and other northern

peoples; the Plains Ojibway moved out of the forests to pursue a buffalo-hunting way of life; and the southern Ojibway supplemented their hunting and gathering with horticulture. The Ojibway of the boreal forests produced one of the most striking and enduring forms of art and religious expression on the continent: red-ochre rock paintings, scattered across the great granite cliffs lining the endless waterways of the Canadian Shield, from northwest Manitoba to eastern Ontario. Because the Ojibway avoided removal, they continue to occupy their traditional homelands in a large number of reservations and other communities in Ontario, Manitoba, Saskatchewan, Michigan, Wisconsin, Minnesota, North Dakota and Montana. (See also NEW MYTHOLOGIES, THE DARK SIDE)

THE OKANAGAN are a Salishan-speaking people who lived in the Plateau region of southern British Columbia and northern Washington. Okanagan dialects include those spoken by the northern and southern groups and by neighbouring SANPOIL, COLVILLE and Lake tribes. The Okanagan were a forest people who fished for salmon, trout, sturgeon and other species along the many lakes and rivers draining the rugged mountain ranges of the area. They hunted deer and other game, and

ROCK PAINTINGS at Darky Lake, in the Quetico region of northern Ontario, capture the essence of traditional and recent Ojibway life. In one scene, several canoes, probably carrying moose hunters, cross the lake in the grip of Mishipizheu. On another part of the rock, a stick figure representing a hunter fires a gun – the puff of smoke suggests that it is an old muzzle-loader. Most importantly, there is a diminutive, but powerful, image of a turtle, which, the Ojibway believe, holds up the earth.

gathered berries, roots and other plants. Some continue to live on ancestral lands, but others fled to the Colville Reservation in Washington to escape harassment by the miners who poured into the area in the late 19th century in search of gold and other metals.

OLD MAN, the TRANSFORMER of the HAN, Dogrib and CHIPEWYAN peoples, outwitted giants, monsters and various animals, including BEAR and WOLVERINE, who all wanted to trap and eat him. RAVEN was his great adversary.

OLD MAN COYOTE is a CROW name for the creator.

THE OMAHA people are a Siouan-speaking tribe who migrated from the prairies and woodlands south of the Great Lakes to settle in the eastern Great Plains, between the Mississippi and Missouri Rivers. They lived in earthlodges (see LODGE) in large villages along the rivers and streams, and grew corn (maize), beans and squash on the region's fertile flood plains, hunted buffalo and other game, and gathered wild plants as the seasons provided. They were traditional allies of the PAWNEE. The Omaha was always a small tribe, with approximately 2,800 members in 1780 but, by 1802, disease and warfare had reduced this already number to 300. Today they occupy a small reservation in northeastern Nebraska, within the limits of their original territories.

IN A HEROIC tale, told by an Omaha story-teller about 100 years ago, two warriors were chasing some Pawnee who had stolen their horses, when they encountered and killed a monstrous rattlesnake. When they ate the monster, they turned into harmless grass snakes that, ever after, came into Omaha camps in the summer.

ONE-WHO-GRABS-BREASTS

see *BEGOCIDI.*

ONEIDA, ONONDAGA

see *IROQUOIS.*

THE ORPHEUS MYTH is a universal theme in which a man (Orpheus, in the original Greek tragedy) journeys to the land of the dead to retrieve his loved one, finds her and begins to lead her out, but loses her to the dead again when he breaks a rule that he must not look at her or touch her on the way back (see under *COYOTE*).

The Chiricahua *APACHE* believe that a critically ill person may enter the underworld and find where their dead ancestors dwell but, if it is not yet their time, they will not eat any food offered to them, and so will return to the world above and recover.

THE OTTAWA people are a Great Lakes Algonquian tribe who lived around Lake Huron, where they hunted game, fished and gathered in a rugged land of granite-edged lakes and rivers, covered by forests. They are close relatives of the *OJIBWAY*, with whom they share a history of migrating from the Atlantic to their present home. Their great chief Pontiac fomented a rebellion in 1763, influenced by a seer known only as the Delaware Prophet, who preached a rejection of the *WHITE MAN* and a return to traditional ways. With the collusion of the French, Pontiac organized all the tribes of the region into a confederacy and over-whelmed many British forts that year, but a long and unsuccessful siege at Detroit eventually proved his downfall. The Ottawa peoples in Canada share two reserves in their traditional lands in Ontario with the Ojibway, whereas the Ottawa in the United States were first removed to northeastern Oklahoma, and were then reset-tled on a small reservation in northern Michigan.

THE PAIUTE [Northern, Southern] are an Uto-Aztecan hunting and gathering people who once occupied a vast territory extending all the way from central Oregon through parts of California and eastwards across the Great Basin as far as southeastern Wyoming.

The Northern Paiute, also called Paviotso, ranged across the desert steppes east of the Cascade Mountains in the north to the Sierra Nevada in the south. Those groups who lived along the shores of lakes subsisted mainly on fish (which they netted and trapped) and waterfowl, along with wild plants, while other bands hunted antelope, deer and other game, and gathered piñon nuts. Miners, loggers and settlers gradually forced them off their lands during the 19th century, although not before there had been a series of battles with the United States military between 1858 and 1868. The tribe finally settled on reservations established in Nevada and Oregon. Many members, however, remained on their ancestral lands in northeastern California, where their descendants now have several small land-holdings. These Cali-

AN IMAGINARY SCENE of prehistoric life in the deserts of the Great Basin, the home of the Paiute. In a world without boundaries, these hardy people chose to remain in this arid, rocky land, and developed a culture successful enough to spread over the present-day states of Nevada, Utah, Arizona and New Mexico.

fornia people, the Owens Valley Paiute, had a similar hunting and gathering way of life in this arid region, but they were able to use irrigation along the Owens River to improve the growing conditions of wild plants that they harvested for their bulbs.

The Southern Paiute are speakers of a language closely related to that of the *UTE.* They once hunted and gathered in a large territory that included parts of present-day California, Arizona, Nevada and Utah. In this harsh and rugged land of semi-desert scrub, they lived mainly on small game and desert plants. The Southern Paiute are culturally distinct from their Northern relatives, and the two groups' languages are mutually unintelligible. After losing most of their population and lands during the late 19th-century occupation of the region by miners and ranchers, the Southern Paiute dispersed into a number of small tribal groups, including the Moapa, and now live in southern Nevada.

PALÖNGAWHOYA see under *POQANGWHOYA BROTHERS.*

THE PAPAGO, or Tohono O'Odham, were desert pastoralists who traditionally occupied the interior of the Sonoran Desert in southwest Arizona. They successfully adapted to the rigours of a hot and dry land by harvesting cacti and other plants, supplemented by hunting birds and other small game. They speak an Uto-Aztecan language closely related to that of the *PIMA*, who live along the nearby Salt and Gila Rivers. Both groups may be descended from the Hohokam, a sophisticated prehistoric culture with the engineering skills needed to construct networks of irrigation canals for their dry valley fields. The Tohono O'Odham now live on three reservations within their aboriginal territory.

A PAPAGO woman. (PHOTOGRAPH BY EDWARD CURTIS, 1907.)

P

PÁPAKALANÓSIWA (*KWAKI-UTL*), a cannibal being associated with the origin of the Hamatsa, a Kwakiutl *SECRET SOCIETY*. The Hamatsa conduct one of the most important dance rituals of the Tsetseka, an extended period of winter ceremonials.

In one version, this fierce monster kidnapped a chief's wife and forced her into an unholy marriage. The chief's three sons eventually found her in Pápakalanósiwa's house, and discovered that she had given birth to a monster son. They fled, but their mother alerted the cannibal, and he chased after them, blowing his whistle and shouting "Hap! Hap! Hap!" (the traditional cry of the Hamatsa dancer). The young men attempted to slow down Pápakalanósiwa with various obstacles. One threw down a stone, which became a mountain; another dropped a comb, which turned into a thicket; a kelp bladder of oil that became a lake; and a stick that became a huge cedar. When they reached the safety of their house, the chief promised the cannibal he would kill his three sons and serve them as food if the monster brought back his wife. When Pápakalanósiwa returned home, he and his son fell into a fire trap and were consumed. With Pápakalanósiwa's death, the chief's wife came to her senses, fanned the ashes and created mosquitoes – condemned to seeking human blood. All that remained of Pápakalanósiwa was the whistle, which has become an important part of the Hamatsa dance.

THE PASSAMAQUODDY people are an Algonquian tribe who once lived along the coastal rivers of north-eastern Maine and adjoining parts of New Brunswick. Theirs was a typical maritime life, fishing and gathering shellfish along the Atlantic shore, and hunting moose, deer, fish and other game on inland rivers and lakes. Once Europeans occupied the coasts,

however, they were forced inland. They were part of the *WABANAKI* confederacy during the 18th century, but they surrendered title to their lands in 1794 and now have a very small reservation (91 ha/225 acres) on Passamaquoddy Bay and a larger parcel of reservation and Federal trust lands in the interior.

PAVAYOYKYASI (*HOPI*) is a being who walks about sprinkling the plants in Hopi fields early every morning with dew. He is envisaged as a handsome youth who always dresses nicely.

PAVIOTSO see under *PAIUTE*.

THE PAWNEE [Chaui, Kitkahahki, Pitahawirata, Skidi] are a Caddoan-speaking people who once ranged through the central Great Plains in Nebraska, Kansas and Oklahoma. They were skilled horticulturalists, growing many varieties of corn (maize), beans and squash, and they hunted buffalo.

A SKIDI PAWNEE chief is wearing a fine buffalo robe, emblazoned with the sacred star symbols that infused all aspects of Pawnee life.

The four Pawnee bands were driven from their lands to a reservation in Oklahoma but, in 1893, the reservation was dissolved in favour of individual land allotments. This shattered a people who, a century earlier, had numbered some 10,000, and by 1906 there were only 600 Pawnee left. The return of some tribal lands in Oklahoma and an improving economic picture has brought the tribe back from the brink of extinction, although its once rich ceremonial culture is now lost. (See also *THE LIVING SKY*)

PAXOJE see *IOWA*.

THE PENOBSCOT people are an Algonquian tribe who, like their more northerly neighbours, the *PASSAMAQUODDY*, lived along coastal rivers in Maine. It is a varied environment, with forests in the north and grasslands in the south. The tribal name is a shortened version of what they call themselves, which translates as "people of the white rocks country". They moved from interior to coast in a seasonal rhythm, hunting moose, deer, beaver and other game, fishing for salmon, sturgeon and other species, gathering shellfish, collecting maple sap and digging the roots of wild plants. Although hundreds of years of acculturation have severely reduced the number of those who speak the native language and practise traditional ways, the tribe continues to protect and nurture what remains. The tribe joined the *WABANAKI* confederacy during the 18th century, but lost most of its territory in 1796, and most of what it had left

THE PEYOTE cactus (Lophophora williamsii), seen here at a site near Huizache, San Luis Potosi, Mexico.

in 1833. It fought back in the courts and, in 1980, a land-claim settlement provided the money to buy property to augment its small reservation and other land-holdings.

PEOPLE MOTHER (Northern *PAIUTE*) figures in a Great Basin human-origins story.

During the time of animal people, a monster that killed with its gaze invaded a village, leaving everyone dead except a small boy and a woman who was living in seclusion outside the village because she was menstruating. She fled with the child, but when she made camp, a giant kidnapped and killed the boy, and displayed the child's body on its belt. The woman sought shelter with Gopher Woman and prepared food for her continuing journey, gathering and grinding seeds into meal. Next, a monstrous *FLYING HEAD* attacked her, but Wood Rat hid her in his cave. Finally, she found the boy, revived him, and they reached the mountain-top home of a hunter, who became her husband. Their union created all the people of the world.

PEYOTE is a hallucinogenic cactus used as a sacrament by the Native American Church.

In a Brule *SIOUX* account of its origin, the *COMANCHE*, a tribe living far to the south in a land of deserts and mesas, suffered from a deadly disease. An old woman dreamed she would find a

MEDICINE herb that would save her people and so, with her granddaughter, she went into the desert to find this magical plant. As night fell, and they huddled together, tired and hungry, she heard the wing-beats of a giant bird. It was an EAGLE, flying on a path from east to west. She prayed to the eagle for wisdom and power, and then, near dawn, she saw a man floating in the air above them. He pointed to a peyote plant, and they discovered that the juice was refreshing.

The second night, he came again, and she prayed for help to get back to her people. This time he told her she would return after two more days with the power to cure. The grandmother and child ate more of the sacred medicine, and power entered the grandmother through it, giving knowledge, understanding and a sacred vision. Although they stayed awake all night, when the sun rose and shone upon the hide bag with the peyote, the woman felt strong. She told her granddaughter to pray to the herb, as it was telling her many things.

On the third night, the spirit came again, and taught her how to show her people the proper way to use the medicine. As she began to wonder how she would find more of this powerful herb, she heard small voices calling – it was all the peyote growing around them. They gathered the peyote buttons and filled the bag. The next night, at sunset, they saw the spirit again, and he pointed the way home. Amazingly, the woman and child had taken no food or drink for four days, yet the peyote kept them strong.

When they returned to their village, they taught the men how to use the herb. The knowledge and wisdom they gained showed them how to gather the sacred things needed for the first peyote altar – the peyote buttons, drum, gourd, fire, water and cedar – and how to make the symbols and conduct the ceremony. They soon conquered the disease, and word of the peyote

ceremony and its great power spread quickly across the continent.

THE PIMA, a horticultural people speaking an Uto-Aztecan language, live along the Gila and Salt Rivers in the Sonoran Desert of southwest Arizona. As with their relatives, the Tohono O'Odham (see PAPAGO), they are probably descendants of the Hohokam, a prehistoric culture who irrigated the desert to grow their crops (see ELDER BROTHER). They raised cotton, corn (maize) and other crops and supplemented their diet with small game and desert plants, including prickly pear, saguaro and other cactus fruits. They are now well known for their fine coiled baskets. The Pima moved to reservations on each of the two rivers in the late 19th century.

PIPES used for smoking tobacco in ritual contexts are treasured sacred objects among many hunting and gathering tribes, as their use manifests the personal and collective relationship between people and the spirit world. The "Peace Pipe", described in historical sources and popular accounts, records only one of the pipe's functions, as a gesture of conciliation and a symbol of common purpose and agreement. To the ARAPAHO, the world as we know it rests on a pipe (see FLAT PIPE) and, to some other Plains cultures, the most powerful spirits gave the pipe as a gift to human beings, as WHITE-BUFFALO-CALF WOMAN gave hers to the

A PIMA BASKET TRAY, woven from willow rods, bleached yucca and, for the black fibres, devil's claw (Proboscidea parviflora), a common cactus-like herb. The design was not mere decoration: it would have had a name and symbolic significance expressing some aspect of Pima religious iconography.

Lakota SIOUX. Loss or neglect of these pipes would be so disastrous that each tribe has keepers who very carefully protect them.

THE PLEIADES is a small, compact constellation of stars visible in the northern hemisphere. Because it appears in the winter, northern tribes associate it with food shortages and other stresses. Central and southern tribes, on the other hand, tend to focus on its origins.

The IROQUOIS incorporate the stars in a lesson about giving respect to your elders. During a pleasant autumn, seven children met daily in a quiet spot on a lake to dance. An old man had warned them that to continue with their

dancing would cause evil, but they persisted and eventually danced into the sky. In a variant, one of them falls back (hence the dim seventh star) and grows as a pine tree, which is why Iroquois relate pine pitch to starlight. The CHEROKEE have a similar story. The YUROK see the stars as six maidens who dance across the sky. The PAWNEE call them the Seven Stars and see them as a symbol of unity.

A NEZ PERCE account offers another explanation for the dim seventh star. One of the seven sister stars, called Eyes-in-Different-Colours, loved an earth man, even after his death, and she mourned so much for him that her eyes became dim with grief and shame. To hide herself away, she took the veil from the sky and covered her face with it.

The NAVAJO depict the PLEIADES (dilyéhé) in string figures. SPIDER WOMAN taught them this art to help them learn to concentrate. The Navajo make this particular figure in order to maintain the clarity necessary to keep things stable and beautiful – the ingredients of a long and fruitful life. (See also THE LIVING SKY, DEATH & AFTERLIFE)

THE PLEIADES is a star cluster in the constellation Taurus. Seven stars are visible to the naked eye, and under clear, very dark conditions, this number increases considerably. Because the cluster is so distinctive, it features in the astronomical observations and mythologies of peoples across the northern hemisphere.

POKANGS is the English name for the *POQANGWHOYA BROTHERS*, the *HOPI* version of the *TWIN* war gods.

POLARIS (Skidi *PAWNEE*), the North Star, is called Karariwari in the Pawnee language – "the star that does not move". Because all the other stars revolve around Karariwari, they consider it to be the Chief Star. He is able to communicate with the chief of the people, ensuring the stability and control necessary to be a strong leader. Near Karariwari is a circlet of stars (the Corona Borealis) known as the Chief's Council.

To the *NAVAJO*, Polaris is the symbolic centre of the hogan (the traditional Navajo home, a conical structure made of logs and sticks and covered with mud, sods or *adobe*); it represents the central fire. They also recognize the Male Revolver (the Plough or Big Dipper) and Female Revolver (Cassiopeia) as elders who set a moral example for earth people. Just as they revolve around Polaris, so people should always be near their homes to carry out family responsibilities.

POLARIS remains fixed in its northern abode, whereas other stars appear to move through the heavens as the earth goes through its seasons. Since the earth moves through a 26,000-year cycle called precession, the true north celestial pole shifts among the northern stars. In ancient times, Thubian was the northern star and, in the distant future, it will be Vega.

THE ACOMA PUEBLO, perched on a massive sandstone mesa that rises a long way above the desert plains of New Mexico, is said to be the oldest inhabited settlement in the United States. Archaeological evidence suggests that the Pueblo built it in the 12th century. The Spanish explorer Coronado visited the site in 1540.

POQANGWHOYA BROTH-ERS (*HOPI*), grandsons of *SPIDER WOMAN*, are the *TWIN* war gods responsible for ridding the world of monsters. The common name is also the elder twin's name; the younger is Palöngawhoya. They tend to be described as ragged and mischievous, and are ardent shinny players (a popular *STICK-AND-BALL GAME*). They normally reside near a Hopi village, although they can roam the world. Their present task is to hold the Earth tightly on each side. If they let go, it will spin wildly.

POSAYAMO, also known as Montezuma, figures in millenarian cults that sprang up after centuries of oppression by whites in Arizona and New Mexico. In some pueblos, people kept sacred fires burning in anticipation of his return to deliver the people from the conquering whites. The Tewa *PUEBLO* say he was born to a virgin who got pregnant while she was eating pine nuts. Although an outcast as a child, he had a spirit father who told him he would one day rule all the Indians, but he left for the south and has not yet returned.

The *PIMA* people had a *CREATION* story in which Montezuma replaced the traditional supernatural, *ELDER BROTHER*.

THE POTAWATOMI once shared the woodlands and prairies south of the Great Lakes with other Algonquian tribes, growing corn (maize), beans and squash, hunting, fishing and gathering wild foods. White occupation of the region in the 18th century devastated the tribe, and they were forcibly relocated to reservation lands in the southern plains of Kansas and Oklahoma. Some groups resisted the removal and instead scattered through northern Indiana, Michigan, northern Wisconsin and Ontario, where they still live. The Potawatomi are traditionally regarded as the "Keeper of the Fire", representing the sacred fire of traditional religion, in the "Three Fires", an alliance with two other related Algonquian tribes. The southern *OJIBWAY* (Chippewa) are the "Keeper of the Faith", and the *OTTAWA* (or Odawa) are the "Keeper of the Trade".

THE PUEBLO [Eastern, Western] people are a diverse group of agrarian cultures who occupy desert regions of the southwest in Arizona and New Mexico. They derive from prehistoric cultures who began cultivating corn (maize) approximately 4,000 years ago and had village sites at least 2,000 years ago. Their other major crops were beans, squash and cotton. The name "Pueblo" derives from a Spanish term meaning "village", describing their characteristic single-storey surface dwellings and multi-storey cliff dwellings of *adobe* (mud brick) or stone. They also build a distinctive underground chamber, the *KIVA*, within which the most important religious rites take place.

The Western Pueblos are the *HOPI*, an Uto-Aztecan tribe, and the *ZUNI*, who speak a language isolate (unrelated to any other known language) that some linguists theorize may be part of the Penutian family. The Eastern Pueblos, settled in the Rio Grande Basin, are the Keres-speaking Keres and *COCHITI*, and the Kiowa-Tanoan groups Tewa, Tiwa and Towa (the Isleta and Taos

Pueblos are Tiwa groups). The Spaniards profoundly influenced the Pueblos, who first came into contact with them in the 16th century, but their well-structured societies and strong defensive force were fairly resistant to assimilation. They continue to live on reservations constituting a small portion of their original homelands. (See also THE DARK SIDE)

PULEKUKWEREK (YUROK) translates as "of downstream (end of world)" and "sharp (horn on buttocks)". A hero and monster-slayer, he introduced the people to true tobacco. Previously they had smoked bay leaves.

A RAINBOW is often assumed to be a positive phenomenon, as it is in Christian iconography. Yet agricultural peoples may see it as a negative sign. The HOPI, for example, say it is an evil force, with a stench so terrible that clouds are afraid of it. If a rainbow arches under clouds on their way to water Hopi lands, the clouds retreat, causing drought.

RAVEN, the major supernatural figure across the northwestern part of the continent, is a hero, TRANSFORMER and TRICKSTER.

For the Alaskan INUIT, Raven created the mainland by harpooning a giant sea animal, without a beginning or end, which then turned into land. The Kobuk say that Raven created land after a great flood by spearing a floating sod of earth, which then sank. He managed to haul it back up into his boat and kill it, at which point it turned into earth.

On the northern Northwest Coast, Raven is the primary hero among the TLINGIT, HAIDA and TSIMSHIAN. In the southern part of the area, his role as transformer is more important. Raven tended to be preoccupied with hunger, and his selfish obsession often led to events crucial to the survival of

ACOMA PUEBLO rainbow dancers wait to perform at an inter-tribal ceremonial in Gallup, New Mexico. At Acoma, the rainbow dance is held during the Christmas season.

humankind. In a Tsimshian narrative, Raven came down from the sky to a village on the southern tip of the Queen Charlotte Islands to complain about the intense mourning of a couple grieving for their dead son. He appeared as a young man, bright as fire, above the boy's bed. The parents hoped that he had come to replace their boy, but – strangely – he did

A TLINGIT RAVEN rattle, collected c. 1850. A kingfisher sits on the top of the rattle, sticking its tongue into the mouth of a human with a bear's head (possibly a mask), and a frog-like creature clings to the raven's belly. Chiefs used these rattles during coming-of-age ceremonies to confer intellectual light, wisdom and the power of the clan on the initiates.

not eat. Then he saw two slaves who ate great quantities of food: a male and female, both named Mouth at Each End. They served the youth a dish of whale meat with a scab in it (which is how the slaves got so hungry), and this made him so ravenous that he ate up all the village's provisions. Ashamed of being unable to satisfy his guest, the chief named him Wigyét (giant), gave him a bladder filled with seeds and told him to fly to the mainland and sow berries on the hillsides and fish-eggs in the streams, so that he would always have something to eat. On the way, he dropped a round stone into the water so he could rest, and it became an island that is seen to this day. After scattering fish-eggs and berries, Wigyét decided it would be easier to get food if the sky was not so dark. The account ends with a theft-of-daylight story (see FIRE for other fire-theft accounts). Thereafter,

people called him Chémsen (raven).

In another Tsimshian narrative, Raven is responsible for DEATH. He came upon Stone and Elderberry, arguing over who should give birth first. He touched Elderberry, and that is why people die and elderberries grow on their graves. If he had touched Stone first, people would exist for ever, just as stones do.

In another story, he provides a lesson in the need to follow ritual correctly. In human form, he took a beautiful woman as his wife. She was the Mistress of Salmon for, when she dipped her fingers into the water, salmon appeared. Raven made a big mistake, using salmon vertebrae as a comb (they must be returned to the water to ensure the immortality of the species) and, when it got stuck in his hair, he cursed the comb. Offended, the salmon wife swam away, forever making the salmon more difficult to catch. (See also TRANSFORMATION, THE TRICKSTER.)

RAVEN AMULETS are worn by INUIT to encourage success in hunting. The inland Netsilik and the Iglulik make amulets of raven claws for male children and attach them to the back-pouches where mothers carry babies. The Iglulik sometimes stitch raven skins into male infants' clothing.

ROCK see INYAN.

R

THE STRANGERS

EVENTS THAT SHAKE UP THE WORLD are preserved in oral tradition. The Micmac tell of a strange, floating "island" that suddenly appeared in the sea. From a distance, the people could see animals climbing in the branches of several trees. When the island drew close the animals became men, and soon a shore party arrived that included a man in the long robes of a priest. These strangers had other wonders in store, such as guns, iron and copper kettles, and woollen blankets. Despite the European origin of such things, each tribe developed stories to explain them within its own traditions. So the Navajo thank their Creator for bringing horses, cattle and sheep from the Spanish in Mexico. As Europeans became more numerous, story-tellers absorbed them into their tales – for example, involving them in the antics of Coyote and other tricksters. But it was the deadly impact of these invaders, and the heroic resistance of native people,

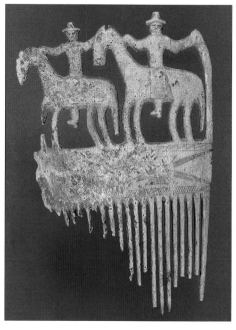

that preoccupied the story-tellers. Thus, the Kiowa culture hero Saynday tricked Smallpox, the bringer of death, into first visiting their traditional enemy, the Pawnee. Before Smallpox could return, Saynday created a ring of fire to protect his people from this terrible scourge.

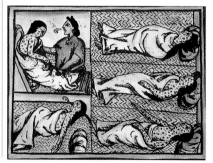

AN IROQUOIAN ornamental hair comb (above) was made from bone by a Cayuga carver in the late 17th century. Traditionally, the decorations were figures associated with Iroquoian life, so this craftsman duly recorded the coming of the white man – probably two European traders arriving at his village in upstate New York.

THE MOST DEVASTATING IMPACT (left) of the European expansion into North America occurred before most native people had ever seen a white man. In 1520, some of the soldiers in the expeditionary force of the Spanish explorer Cortés suffered from smallpox, a disease that had ravaged the Far East and then Europe for at least 2,000 years. As the native people had no resistance against this and other common European diseases, it moved quickly through the Aztec population in Mexico and then spread across North America, killing millions. (ILLUSTRATION BY A 16TH-CENTURY AZTEC ARTIST.)

A MILITARY EXPEDITION (left) in 1874, led by General George Armstrong Custer, discovered gold in the Black Hills of Dakota Territory, land sacred to the Sioux. The predictable flood of prospectors and miners on to Sioux lands precipitated a series of bitter conflicts with the military who, despite treaty obligations, defended white interests. On 25 June 1876, Custer's Seventh Cavalry attempted to put down a force of Sioux, Northern Cheyenne and Northern Arapaho warriors along the Little Big Horn River. Famously, they failed, and were completely wiped out. This coloured pencil drawing, made by one of the Sioux combatants, records the action in the heat of the battle.

THE INTRODUCTION of the horse (right) was responsible for the transformation of Great Plains culture. Because of the vast distances across the grasslands, most groups living in the region were river-bound horticulturalists. When hunting and gathering tribes from the South, the Great Lakes region and the western mountains obtained the horse, however, they were able to move across the plains and hunt the buffalo. In this picture, Osage warriors round up wild horses. (PAINTING BY GEORGE CATLIN, 19TH CENTURY.)

THE MICMAC (below) were skilled sea hunters who pursued whales and porpoises in canoes specifically designed for ocean travel. When the French and English introduced sailing vessels into the region, the Micmac adapted them easily to their own use. Micmac, hunting and fishing along the shores of Kejimkujik Lake, in south-central Nova Scotia, engraved the smooth slate shoreline rocks with images of their culture – here, two seagoing canoes with masts and sails, are steered by men wearing European top hats, which were a popular trade item in the 19th century.

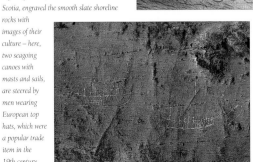

A DETAIL (left) of the Sioux drawing of the battle of the Little Big Horn River, showing a warrior striking down a Seventh Cavalry trooper.

S

SAC see *FOX*.

SAHTU see *DENE*.

THE SALISH [Coast, Interior] are named after their Salishan language. The Coast Salish occupy the coastal areas of southern British Columbia and southeastern Vancouver Island, and the northern coasts of the Olympic Peninsula in Washington. They had no agriculture, but the warm Pacific coastal environment provided them with an abundance of sea and forest resources, including whales and other sea mammals, salmon, oolichan and other salt-water fish, trout, clams, mussels, sea urchins and other shellfish, deer, bear and other game of the temperate rainforests, and a wide range of wild plants. Since they had a food surplus, they adopted a sedentary lifestyle, living in villages of cedar-plank houses, and developed a complex social organization – including a stratified society with nobles, commoners and slaves – resembling those of agricultural peoples. They produced art in abundance, mainly depictions of mythological ancestors representing *CLAN* and family crests, on carved and painted cedar *TOTEM POLES* as well as on a wide range of ceremonial and household goods. Although they now have only a small portion of their original territory, they continue to live in the lands of their ancestors. For more information about the Interior Salish, see *FLATHEAD*.

SALMON BOY (*HAIDA*) offended salmon and was taken to the land of the salmon people. He learned the rituals that fishers must use when they catch salmon, returned briefly as a human to teach his people these rituals, and then went back to live with the salmon for ever.

SALT WOMAN (*COCHITI*) created salt from her flesh and mucus.

As salt is crucial to Southwestern peoples, those seeking it must conduct detailed rituals and observe strict taboos.

SALTEAUX see under *OJIBWAY*.

THE SANPOIL people are an Interior Salishan tribe, speaking a dialect of the *OKANAGAN* language, who live in the Columbia Plateau region of northern Washington. Like other tribes that inhabit this rugged region of grass-covered valleys, forested hills and mountain ranges, the Sanpoil were mainly fishers and hunters. They now share the Colville Reservation in northeastern Washington (established in 1872) with a bewildering mix of other small Plateau tribes.

SAPLING see under *FLINT*.

SALMON, when they are ready to spawn, swim up the fast-flowing rivers in vast numbers until they reach the place of their own birth, a bed of freshwater gravel. During this journey, they can be speared as they leap through rapids and narrow channels on their way upstream, as this modern impression of a Chinook fisherman shows. (PAINTING BY ERNST BERKE.)

THE SARCEE, who prefer to be known as the Tsuu T'ina, are an Athapascan people of the northern Great Plains, occupying southern and central Alberta. They were traditionally allied with two Algonquian tribes, the *BLACKFOOT* and the *GROS VENTRE*, in the Blackfoot Confederacy. They pursued the traditional Plains life of buffalo hunting until disaster struck. First, a smallpox epidemic devastated them in 1869 and 1870. Then, white hunters began to slaughter the buffalo for their hides, leaving few for the Sarcee. After a drought in 1878, when the buffalo migrated to better grasslands south of the US border, white hunters set prairie fires to prevent their return north again. This caused the virtual extinction of the buffalo in Canada by 1879, and collapse of the buffalo-hunting cultures soon afterwards. Having lost their livelihood

and source of food, the Sarcee were at the mercy of the Canadian government. They now occupy a small reserve in southern Alberta.

SAUK see *FOX*.

SAYA see *YAMANHDEYA*.

SAYNDAY is the *KIOWA CULTURE HERO* and *TRICKSTER*. In one of his most notable exploits, he arranged the theft of the sun from the far side of the world to quell the eternal darkness among his own people. He first kept the sun in front of his *LODGE*, where it burned too brightly, and then inside, where its light was so intense it shone through the walls, and finally on the roof, above the smoke-hole. This caused a fire that destroyed the lodge, and so he threw the sun away, into the sky.

SEA MOTHER (*INUIT*) is generally known as Sedna in the central

A SHAMAM of the Southern Ojibway tribe incised this plan view of part of a Midéwegan, the sacred Midé lodge, on a birch-bark scroll at Leech Lake, Minnesota. It depicts Mishipizheu and the other manitous through whom the shamans draw their curing power.

and eastern Arctic, among the Mackenzie, Copper, Netsilik, Iglulik and Baffin Island groups. Present in the sea and all its animals, she is the MISTRESS OF ANIMALS and MOTHER OF ANIMALS.

Story-tellers sometimes recount her origin in a singular narrative, and sometimes in an extension of the DOG HUSBAND story. A woman, the "one who would have no children" married, but she was miserable. As the winter ended, her father visited and decided to take her back. When her husband discovered what had happened, he turned into a seabird (identified as a petrel or fulmar) and flew after them. As he neared the fleeing pair, he caused a great storm that tossed the boat around so violently that the girl fell overboard. She clung to the gunwale, but the father cut off her fingers. They fell into the water and became different animal species: seals, walrus, whales, salmon and polar bears (depending on the version). The fingerless woman then sank to the bottom of the sea and became Sea Mother.

People respect her through hunting ritual, taboos and the ritual disposal of sea-mammal and fish remains. When they observe the proper rituals, she responds by providing abundant game and fish, and when they neglect the rituals, she takes away those resources. In order to counter the threat of star-vation, SHAMANS then have to go into trances to comb Sedna's hair, infested with the vermin of broken taboos – as she is without fingers, she cannot comb it herself. When they finish, she is grateful, and sets the game animals free again.

SECRET SOCIETIES are social organizations with an exclusive membership (most often determined by sex, age and social status), a hierarchical structure and a set of esoteric beliefs and rituals, which are generally devoted to religious matters responsible for the health and welfare of the group. They are most commonly found in agrarian cultures (and, in modern times, industrialized ones), where the economic and power structures exist to maintain a system in which individuals may be differentiated by social status. The Flute and Snake societies of PUEBLO peoples are examples of the many secret societies among agricultural groups in North America. The prosperous hunters and gatherers of the Northwest Coast have secret societies in which membership is confined to élites and may be inherited. The MIDÉWIWIN of the OJIBWAY and other Algonquians of the Great Lakes region was a secret curing society of SHAMANS.

SEDNA See under SEA MOTHER.

SEMINOLE DANCERS, wearing traditional dress of multicoloured cotton, perform in front of a chickee, a stilt house open on all four sides and thatched with palmetto leaves.

THE SEMINOLE consist of members of related Muskogean tribes dispersed by waves of European incursion and expansion beginning in the 15th century.

These tribes hunted, fished, gathered and grew crops in the richly varied environments of Florida. Most Seminole are descended from the CREEK, who once occupied a vast territory in the southeast. The present tribal character and distribution came about during and after the Seminole Wars, a protracted resistance to forced removal fought in the Everglades between 1835 and 1842. In 1830, President Andrew Jackson signed the Indian Removal Act, which forced the removal of all tribes west of the Mississippi River. The CHEROKEE won a United States Supreme Court case defending their right to remain, but the President simply ignored the verdict and ordered the United States Army to evict all the affected tribes, including the Seminole, from their ancestral lands. In the ensuing removal and long forced march to Indian Territory (now Oklahoma) known as the Trail of Tears, cruelty by the Army, starvation, disease, harassment by bandits and by hostile western tribes caused wholesale suffering and the decimation of the peoples involved. The Seminole were able to resist because they could hide deep in the swampy reaches of the Everglades, but eventually most were relocated to Oklahoma. Despite the dominance of white society, the tribe maintains its traditional culture in both Florida and Oklahoma.

SENECA see IROQUOIS.

SHAMANS are the religious specialists of hunting and gathering tribes, using spiritual techniques extending back to Palaeolithic times. Theirs is a highly individual ability, involving some form of transcendence to carry them into the spirit world. They may be healers (hence the common term "MEDICINE man"), seers (essential in hunting and warfare), or keepers of sacred knowledge. Although agriculturalists tend to have organized priesthoods, their cultures usually maintain shamanic elements, especially in matters of fertility, hunting magic, and the seeking of visions. (See also TRANSFORMATION, SPIRITS OF THE EARTH, DEATH & AFTERLIFE, THE DARK SIDE.)

SHAMANS on the Northwest Coast conduct a ritual outside a cedar plank house. They wear woven cedar bark blankets. (PHOTOGRAPH BY E.J. CURTIS, 1914.)

THE SHOSHONI [Western, Eastern], a large tribe of Uto-Aztecan speakers, hunted and gathered over a vast territory that included parts of the Great Basin, Plateau and Great Plains, in what is today eastern California, eastern Oregon, central Nevada, southern Idaho, northern Utah and western Wyoming. The Western Shoshoni pursued an exacting seasonal round in their relatively arid and resource-poor territory. They trapped groundhogs and other rodents, sage grouse and other birds, gathered pine nuts, grass seeds and berries, and, in the autumn, organized large communal antelope hunts. They now occupy reserves in Nevada, Idaho and California. The Northern, or Wind River, Shoshoni took to the Plains way of life, subsisting mainly on buffalo. They were settled in the Wind River Reservation in west central Wyoming in 1868.

THE SNAKE RIVER in Wyoming derives its name from an earlier historic name for the Shoshoni people. The Mandan, Omaha and Teton Sioux referred to them as "Snakes" because their tribal sign was a serpentine gesture.

SIERRA MIWOK see YOSEMITE.

SILA (INUIT) is the supreme being of the physical universe, responsible for the winds.

THE SIOUX [Dakota, Lakota, Nakota] people are made up of 14 Siouan-speaking tribes (known

LOW DOG was a warrior chief of the Oglala Sioux, who fought General Custer at the Battle of the Little Big Horn in 1876. He is wearing a bone breastplate and bone necklaces to protect him in battle.

popularly as the Sioux) and had a territory that once extended across the prairies and Plains from Wisconsin to the foothills of the Rocky Mountains in Montana. With their central location in the Plains, they became fully adapted to buffalo hunting, which provided most of their food resources, clothing and other material necessities. The name "Sioux" is no longer preferred, because it derives from an Algonquian pejorative "nadowesiuh", meaning "snakes".

There were originally seven nations in three dialect groups in this territory. The Lakota, known as the Teton, were in the west; the Nakota, comprising the Yankton and Yanktonai, in the centre; and the Dakota, comprising the Mdewakanton, Wahpekute, Sisseton and Wahpeton, were to the east. The Brule people are a subdivision of the Lakota.

These Siouan peoples suffered the fate of all native people in the region, after a heroic resistance against the military lasting for almost 50 years. This included the legendary Battle of the Little Big Horn (often called Custer's Last Stand) on 25 June 1876, when a force of Sioux, Northern CHEYENNE, and Northern ARAPAHO wiped out General George Armstrong Custer and his Seventh Cavalry. The resistance ended with the Seventh Cavalry's catastrophic massacre of Big Foot and his mainly unarmed band of men, women and children at Wounded Knee Creek, in South Dakota, on 29 December 1890. In spite of such depredations, the tribe fiercely retains the essence of its traditional culture and controls significant territory in its homeland, especially in South Dakota. (See also DEATH AND AFTERLIFE, THE STRANGERS, NEW MYTHOLOGIES)

SIPAPU (PUEBLO), the opening into the underworld, is often believed to lie under a lake. The Taos Pueblo emergence lake may be Blue Lake, north of the Taos pueblo itself. The HOPI emerged at Ongtupqa (the Grand Canyon) at a site known as Sipaapuni. They believe that, when people die, they return there. For them, this most

sacred part of Ongtupqa is the dwelling place of KACHINAS, and the source of clouds.

SLAVE, SLAVEY see DENE.

SOLITUDE-WALKER see TAIKOMOL.

SPIDER ROCK (NAVAJO), the home of SPIDER WOMAN, is located in Canyon de Chelly, Arizona.

SPIDER WOMAN is a supernatural being who is common to many oral traditions.

When the first ancestors of the NAVAJO emerged, monsters roamed the lands. Spider Woman (Na ashje'ii 'Asdzáá) gave power to her grandsons, NAYENEZGANI AND TOBADJISHTCHINI, to search for the sun, their father, and ask him for help. When they found him, he showed them how to destroy the monsters. Grandmother Spider eventually became one of the most important Navajo deities, responsible for many of the essential cultural features, including weaving on a loom. When her tasks were finished, she chose the top of SPIDER ROCK for her home.

The HOPI say she was created before animals. She led the first people up from the underworld.

She has two forms – a small spider and an aged, but ageless, grandmother. As a spider, she lives in the ground in a small KIVA-like chamber, and emerges from a hole likened to the SIPAPU. Like all grandmothers, she is wise and compassionate, coming to the aid of people in need or danger.

STAR BOY is a hero (known by various names) among the CROW, ARAPAHO, BLACKFOOT, IOWA and other Plains tribes. His story

generally begins with the tale of the *STAR HUSBAND*.

An old woman, known as Grandmother, Old-Woman-Night, or Old-Woman-Who-Never-Dies adopted the boy. Like *LODGE BOY AND THROWN AWAY*, he was a monster-slayer. At the climax of his adventures, he went through death and resurrection. A snake entered his body, stayed until the boy died, and remained even as he became a pile of bones. Since the snake prevented him from returning to life, he rose into the sky and became the Morning Star. To the Blackfoot, he is the tribal hero, Scarface. The *KIOWA* say that early on the hero divided into two Split Boys. One eventually disappeared under a lake, while the other transformed himself into the *tsaidetali MEDICINE*, which are the sacred bundles, or portable altars, of the Kiowa.

STAR HUSBAND is a popular narrative, found everywhere south of the Arctic, about women who take stars as husbands.

In a Coast *SALISH* version, two sisters who fell in love with the stars rose into the sky, and one bore a son. While digging roots, the sisters accidentally punched a hole in the sky and, seeing the earth below, made a ladder out of twisted cedar boughs, and descended, taking the baby with them. The child was *MOON*. The sisters asked Toad to look after Moon, but she was blind, so Dog Salmon took Moon off to his country at the edge of the world. Moon grew up and had sons of his own. Meanwhile, the sisters created another child from Moon's cedar-bark nappy (diaper). Then Moon began his journey home, accompanied by Dog Salmon. On the way, he transformed beings into stone and into animals and landscape features. When he reached his sky home, he joined his brother, who became the Sun.

STARS and all the major celestial bodies figure in oral traditions. The *ZUNI* join the origin of several stars in an account of the battle between the *TWIN* war gods and Cloud-swallower, who is taking all the clouds from the sky and causing droughts. They cannot defeat him head on, so they join forces with Gopher, who takes them into the earth and tunnels up beneath Cloud-swallower's heart. They shoot the monster and fling his various parts into the sky. His heart flies into the east and becomes the Morning Star, his liver flies west and becomes the Evening Star, his lungs rise as the Seven Stars (*PLEIADES*), and his entrails lie across the sky as the *MILKY WAY*.

STICK-AND-BALL GAMES originated deep in North American prehistory. They were already being played with numerous variations by peoples all across the continent when the first Europeans arrived.

MYRIAD STARS light the dark deserts of Arizona, forming timeless patterns that gave native intellectuals a way to chart the rhythms of life and the vastness of their lands.

CHOCTAW WARRIORS, with playing sticks in each hand, move in a seething mass around the elusive ball, in a stick-and-ball game observed in the early 19th century. (PAINTING BY GEORGE CATLIN.)

Stickball is set on a playing field with goals (posts) at either end. Players – sometimes hundreds – each carry a stick with a small net at the top (the *CHOCTAW*, according to the painter George Catlin, who observed a game in 1836, held a stick in each hand) and attempt to carry, or throw, the ball across the opposing goal line. The modern game of lacrosse, brought to European colonists by the *IROQUOIS*, is a variant of stickball. The sky people play games of stickball in the *ALABAMA* story of the *CELESTIAL CANOE*.

Shinny was another game with a similar structure, except that, in this one, the sticks were curved at the end in order to strike, rather than catch, the ball. It was played by the *HOPI CULTURE HEROES* the *POQANGWHOYA BROTHERS*.

Such games could be fiercely competitive, and indeed they were sometimes violent, but they helped to release tensions between or within tribes, just as sports do in modern cultures. The religious ceremonies that attended such games reveal the seriousness of their intent.

NEW GODS

WHEN THE FIRST CHRISTIAN MISSIONARIES set foot on the North American continent, they found peoples they could not fit into the Biblical history of the world. While these aboriginal cultures had millennia of wisdom and experience, the newcomers saw them as primitive, virtually non-human and in need of correction. As the Europeans explored and occupied native lands, the flood of alien ideas and material goods they generated quickly overwhelmed native cultures already decimated by invasion, the spread of foreign diseases and forced removal from their homelands. These depredations caused drastic changes in their world view. No longer intertwined with their own earth and sky, the natives of the land listened and learned – sometimes avidly, but more often helplessly – about a single god and a morality fashioned on a distant continent. In some places they were also prey to conflicting ideas, as missionaries of different faiths competed for converts. Some groups resisted by creating new narratives to counter Christian teachings. Others attempted to avoid the total loss of their mythologies by appropriating Christian elements, especially a single creator or a Jesus-like transformer who took the place of the traditional culture hero. But, even though more than 400 years of aggressive missionary work has forever altered oral tradition, the spiritual remoteness of the Christian drama allowed the survival of fundamental native beliefs about the spiritual essence of the landscape and its knowing creatures.

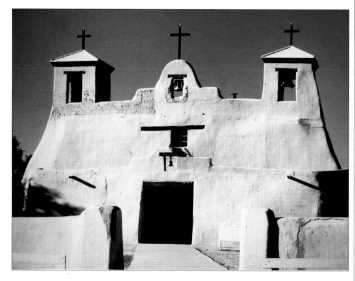

WHEN MISSIONARIES moved into an Indian settlement, they ran the risk of being killed for their aggressive assaults on religious traditions that were many thousands of years older than Christianity. Spanish Franciscan monks built this mission at Isleta Pueblo, New Mexico, in 1629, and fortified it heavily against Indian attacks. Two Franciscan missionaries had been murdered nearby in 1581, and the threat of Pueblo resistance was always tangible.

RELIGIOUS paraphernalia (above) that had a distinctive Micmac style developed after most of the Micmac were converted to Christianity by French Catholic missionaries in the 18th century. Altarpieces in particular were elaborately decorated, as in this petroglyph example, carved in slate at McGowan Lake, in central Nova Scotia.

AN ALTARPIECE (above), painted by Father Guy-Mary Rousselière in a small wooden church on the shore of Pond Inlet, in the Canadian Arctic territory of Nunavut, shows Inuit having a vision of Jesus Christ.

IN A HIDE PAINTING (right), commemorating a late-19th-century Sun Dance, participants gather around a large Christian cross. As Christian beliefs and rituals spread through Indian communities across the continent, they were often integrated into traditional ceremonies as one of the host of powerful forces that had to be respected.

T

THE SUN DANCE, a sacred renewal ceremony, is held throughout the Plains in late spring or early summer. It generally involves four days of complex ritual with allusions to boy heroes such as Scarface for the *BLACKFOOT*, and *LODGE BOY AND THROWN AWAY* for the *HIDATSA*.

The *ARAPAHO* place a special knife on the Sun Dance altar, said to be the one Double Face used when performing a caesarean section on the mother of their *TWIN* heroes (see under *LODGE BOY*). They also honour the mother of *STAR BOY*, identifying her with the centre pole in the Sun Dance lodge. In the Arapaho version of the *STAR HUSBAND* tale, the young heroine climbs a tree into the sky following a porcupine (usually the sun or moon in disguise). (See also *NEW GODS.)*

SWEATLODGE rituals are, even today, an essential part of religious worship in many American Indian cultures. They serve two primary purposes: for ritual cleansing and for the intensification of sensual experience through the effects of intense heat and darkness, which can lead to heightened states of awareness. The most common type of sweatlodge is a small hut, fashioned from curved saplings

and covered with skins or bark. The participants bring hot rocks into the structure from a fire outside and pour water over them, producing the steam. As sweating is a ritual, the construction of the lodge and the carrying out of the sweat follow religious prescriptions and may be attended by songs, prayers and other rituals. In the Great Plains, for example, a sweat is an essential part of the *SUN DANCE* ceremony.

SWEET MEDICINE see *HOOP-AND-POLE GAME.*

THE TAHLTAN are an Athapascan people who lived in the Stikine River region of northern British Columbia, hunting, fishing and gathering in a seasonal round through their remote boreal-forest environment. They continue to pursue many of their traditional ways, but they are now centred in the towns of Telegraph Creek, Dease Lake and Iskut.

TAIKOMOL (*YUKI*) or Solitude-walker, the creator, began as a voice in sea foam, then rose up in human form and established the earth by laying a cross over the water.

TENA see *DENA.*

TEPEES (Tipis) are conical tents of skin (or bark) covering a frame of poles, erected in a circle, that support each other at the apex. An uncovered area at the top serves as a smoke-hole for the tent. Tepees were the characteristic dwellings of the nomadic buffalo-hunting peoples of the Great Plains, but were used by many different North American peoples.

TEWA, TIWA see *PUEBLO.*

THROWN AWAY
see under *LODGE BOY.*

THUNDERBIRD, a giant bird often identified as responsible for thunder and lightning, is a powerful spirit, demanding respect among many peoples.

The *PASSAMAQUODDY* tell of two men who tried to discover the origin of thunder. They travelled north to a high mountain and saw a cave-like opening, which they tried to enter. One made it through but, as the other crossed

the threshold, the mountain closed in, and he died. The survivor walked into a large plain with an encampment of tepees (huts of arched poles covered with bark, animal skin or woven mats, typical of Algonquians of the northeast) and people playing a ball game. As he watched, they finished their game, sprouted wings and flew south – they were thunderbirds. He came upon some old men left in the village, and told them that he wanted to know where thunder came from. They put him into a large mortar and pounded him until he was soft enough to be shaped into a new body: a thunderbird. Then they gave him a bow and arrows, and sent him on his way. Although he was now a thunderbird, he never forgot his homeland, and so he became a powerful protector of the Passamaquoddy tribe. (See also *THE LIVING SKY, THE DARK SIDE*)

ON A PAWNEE ceremonial drum, the *dark leading edge of a prairie storm takes* *the shape of a giant thunderbird. As the* *thunderbird's eyes and wings flash with* *lightning, the winds, rushing into the* *coming storm, stir up a flock of swallows.*

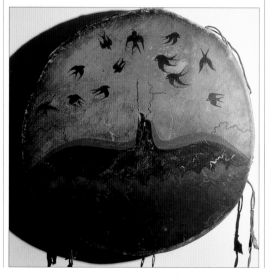

THIS IS A TLINGIT example of a typical shamanic device. Northwest coast shamans sometimes diagnosed an illness as the loss of the patient's spirit or soul. To bring the spirit back they used a small, polished bone carved in the shape of a two-headed animal (usually the sisiutl, a two-headed sea monster) and engraved with a third, central face. The shaman would catch the spirit in this device and then blow it back into the patient's body. This example is inlaid with abalone shell.

TIIKUYWUUTI (*HOPI*) died giving birth, hence her name, Child-Sticking-Out Woman. She is the mother of all game animals. She is beautiful, daubs her face with a white pigment, and wears a mask and a ruffled collar. Unsuccessful hunters pray to her to have intercourse with them, so that they can be better hunters. She leaves behind the tracks of a jack rabbit.

TIRÁWAHAT (*PAWNEE, ARIKARA*), the creator (whose name translates as "expanse") is a powerful, unseen presence residing at the zenith, who puts the gods in their proper places. The Sun occupies the east, the *MOON*, the west. The Morning Star is the warrior who drives *STARS* towards the west, where the Evening Star presides as the mother of all things.

Tiráwahat made a North Star, a Southern Star and other stars to help hold up the sky; then the four elements – Clouds, Winds, Lightning, Thunder (given to the Evening Star to put in her garden); and then the earth. The creator fashioned the earth by first dropping a pebble in a large stormy cloud; water was formed, then the sky-supporters struck the water with their war clubs, separating it

so that earth appeared. When the Evening Star took the Morning Star as her consort, they produced a girl who would be the mother of humanity, and the Moon and Sun produced a boy to be her husband. The new husband learned from Evening Star how to make the sacred *MEDICINE* bundle, and the elements taught him the songs of all the ceremonies.

TLAGU (*TLINGIT*), translated as "of the long ago", is the term Tlingit story-tellers use to refer to stories of the past, including core beliefs and all the forms of story-telling related to the ancients.

THE TLINGIT, speakers of a Na-Dene language, once controlled the coasts of southeast Alaska and northern British Columbia, and the southeastern edge of Yukon Territory. They led a sea-going life, hunting whales and other sea mammals, salmon, halibut and other salt-water fish, clams, mussels and other shellfish, and deer and other forest game. Their culture was similar to the complex and highly structured societies of the *HAIDA* and *TSIMSHIAN* to the south, with an intricate and abundant art and ceremonialism devoted to the display of the mythological ancestors of *CLANS* and families. They occupied areas exploited heavily by Russians, British and Americans during the heyday of the fur trade, but successfully resisted the aggressive and often murderous traders until the purchase of the territory by the United States in 1906. Contact with European and American cultures, however, caused debilitating disease, dislocation and acculturation in the same way that it did among other coastal peoples. Many Tlingit are assimilated into the dominant society, but some

continue to pursue their traditional culture. (See also *TRANSFORMATION, THE LIVING SKY, NEW MYTHOLOGIES*)

TOBACCO see *WYANDOT*.

TOBADJISHTCHINI see *NAYENEZGANI*.

TOHONO O'ODHAM see *PAPAGO*.

TOTEM POLES are monumental cedar poles erected by northern Northwest Coast peoples to display family and *CLAN* crests, denoting their legendary descent from animal ancestors.

The *KWAKIUTL* recount the appearance of the first totem pole. Wakiash was a chief, but he did not own a dance as the other chiefs did, so he went into the mountains to fast in the hopes of gaining one. After four days, a little green frog appeared and told him to lie still, as he was on the back of a raven that would fly him around the world for four days. Among the wonderful things he saw was a house with a beautiful totem pole in front. The frog read his thoughts and told the raven to stop. When the chief came to the entrance of the house, he heard singing. Wakiash caught a little mouse-woman who ran outside, and gave her a piece of mountain-goat fat. When she asked him what he wanted, he demanded the pole, the house and the dances and songs. He then surprised the animals in their dance, which caused them great shame because they were masquerading as humans. To compensate, they taught him their songs and dances, and showed him their masks, including the Echo mask. The Beaver Chief added a special pole he named Kalakuyuwish, meaning sky pole. Beaver folded the house up like a little bundle, gave Wakiash a headdress, and

instructed him to throw down the bundle when he reached home and all would reappear.

Wakiash did as he was told, and the house was wonderful, as all the creatures on it moved. The whale painted on the house front was blowing, the carved animals on the pole spoke in their own languages, and all the masks inside the house talked and cried aloud. This raucous behaviour woke up Wakiash's people. When they came to the chief's house they told him it was not four days but four years that he had been away. Wakiash danced for the people, taught them the songs he had learned and showed them how to use the masks. When at last the dancing stopped, the house disappeared, back to the animals. All the chiefs were envious because Wakiash had the best dance of all. He then made a house and masks and a great totem pole out of wood, which all the people honoured with a new song. This was the first pole – Kalakuyuwish, or the pole that holds up the sky. (See also *NEW MYTHOLOGIES, THE DARK SIDE*)

THIS TOTEM is known as the "Hole-in-the-Sky" pole. It was originally used as the ceremonial entrance point for a house in Kitwancool village, a Tsimshian settlement situated along the banks of Skeena River in British Columbia.

and *RAVEN*, may combine both heroic virtues and a predilection for playing silly, selfish or evil pranks. Others, such as *COTTONTAIL*, never quite rise to the level of the heroic, acting instead as foils or sidekicks to their braver and more gallant companions. (See also *TRANSFORM-ATION, THE TRICKSTER*)

THE TSIMSHIAN [Gitksan, Niska, Tsimshian] consist of three Penutian-speaking tribal groups who occupy the northern coast of British Columbia, extending up the Nass and Skeena River basins into the Coast Mountains. Since their territory included both coasts and mountains, they had access to an enormous variety of natural resources, whales and other sea mammals, salmon, halibut and other salt-water fish, mussels, sea urchins, clams and other shellfish, and deer and other game in the coastal forests. As the Niska and Gitksan lived along the flanks of the Coast Mountains, they were able to hunt mountain sheep and goats, from which they obtained wool that they traded with their coastal relatives in return for oil from the oolichan fish (also known as the candlefish because, when dried, it could be lit like a taper). With a sedentary lifestyle and the ability to

produce and trade surplus food and materials, the tribe developed social structures and traditions more consistent with agricultural-ists than hunters and gatherers. They produced magnificent carv-ings in cedar, from monumental *TOTEM POLES* to intricately fash-ioned boxes and other ceremonial wares, and also carved, painted and engraved horn, copper and other materials, and wove fine baskets. Typical of Northwest Coast peoples, they produced masks depicting their mythological animal ances-tors, but they also created portrait masks of stunning realism. Pro-tected by their resource base, the Tsimshian have survived the worst depredations of European culture, and continue to maintain many of their cultural traditions.

THE TRICKSTER AND TRANSFORM-ER RAVEN finds humankind in a cockle shell, as on this chest lid. It is carved in argil-lite, a dense, dark slate, by Charles Edenshaw, the premier Haida carver of the late 19th century.

TOWA see *PUEBLO*.

TRANSFORMERS are an essen-tial element of American Indian religious philosophy, as these super-natural beings are responsible for the *CREATION* of the world as it is now, in the age of the story-tellers. During the formative age, all beings had the capacity to transform both themselves and things around them, as the entire world was fluid and changing. Hence, both *CUL-TURE HEROES* and villains took part. Some transformations were inten-tional, such as the creation of humans and animals, but some others were incidental, produced in the course of supernatural events. Transformers ensured that all of nature and culture had an origin that fitted logically into the beliefs and traditions of the tribe, securing a clear and powerful sense of social identity. Examples of transformers are the culture heroes *COYOTE*, *RAVEN*, *TIIKUYWUUTI* and *TRAV-ELLER*. (See also *TRANSFORMATION*)

TRAVELLER (*DENA*), a *CULTURE HERO* also known as "the Man-

who-Went-Through Everything" or "the One-who-Travelled-Among-all-the-Animals-and-People", canoed into Dena territory from the head-waters of the Yukon River. Dena peoples living along the Koyukuk River call him "Betohoh", because he became a Pine Grosbeak when he died. His adventures contrast somewhat with *RAVEN*'s because he tended to avoid mischief.

He was a canoe maker. In a Dena version, he experimented until he successfully made a birch-bark canoe. He killed a spruce grouse, took out the breastbone and fitted the bones together for the frame. Then he cut up a sheet of birch bark and got some women to sew it together around the canoe and seal the joins with pitch.

TRICKSTERS are beings with supernatural powers who intro-duce a strong sense of reality into myths, as they manifest the whole range of human foibles, counter-balancing the often idealized and rarefied personalities of gods and *CULTURE HEROES*. Some beings, such as the culture heroes *COYOTE*

TSÚNUKWA (*KWAKIUTL*) is a cannibal, one of the Winter Dance spirits. She can bring the dead to life, but story-tellers represent her as dim-witted.

In one Winter Dance origin story, a young man helped her recover the body of her dead son. After reviving him with her water of life, the grateful mother gave the hero a supply of the water and a mask representing herself, which he later wore in performing the first Tsúnukwa dance.

TSUU T'INA see *SARCEE*.

TUSCARORA see *IROQUOIS*.

THE TUSKEGEE people were a small southeastern tribe, subsisting on hunting, gathering and horti-culture, who lived in what is now north-central Alabama and adjoin-

A SHAMAN'S MASK is carved with the subtlety and fine finishing characteristic of the Tsimshian. The combination of human and animal attributes reflects the shaman's ability to transcend the present world and commune with the animal ancestors.

ing parts of Tennessee. They seemed to have adopted the *CREEK* lan-guage and customs during the late 18th century, and are now extinct.

TWINS are a very common char-acter type in Native American mythology. In the Southwest, the *NAVAJO*, *APACHE*, *PUEBLO* and other tribes characterize warrior twins as *CULTURE HEROES*, working together to transform the world and slay monsters. *LODGE BOY* and his twin brother, Thrown Away, fulfil the same role for the *HIDATSA* in a story cycle of heroic twins that is found throughout the Plains.

Twins can also be used to serve as a metaphor for opposition – such as between good and evil, as in the Iroquoian stories of Sapling and his evil brother *FLINT*.

UPRIVER-OCEAN GIRL (*YU-ROK*) was the provider of water for the Yurok world.

COYOTE searched for water, because the country had none, and he knew humans would need it. He travelled everywhere looking for water, all across the sky, and then decided to go upriver. He crossed the sky, descended to earth on a ladder and met Upriver-Ocean Girl. He told her that there was no water, so she created it out of her body. She entered the dry river bed and the water began to flow into a lake. Coyote pointed out that the water would be no good without fish, so she created salmon and trout.

THE UTE [Ute, Chemehuevi] are speakers of an Uto-Aztecan lan-guage who at one time hunted and gathered across a vast territory in the Great Basin, through Utah and Colorado and into parts of south-ern Wyoming and northern New Mexico. Having access to a variety of environments beyond the arid desert steppes, they were able to supplement their hunting of ante-lope and rabbits with deer, elk, buffalo and mountain sheep. Where available, they also caught fish and reptiles, trapped wildfowl, and gathered edible insects. After numerous forced removals, reloca-tions and the eventual loss of most of their reservation lands, the three dialect groups, the Ute, Southern *PAIUTE*, and Chemehuevi, are now settled on reservations in southeast Colorado and eastern and north-eastern Utah.

THE WABANAKI ("daybreak land people") confederacy, was an alliance of several eastern Algon-quian hunting and gathering tribes inhabiting the Atlantic coasts and the interior from Nova Scotia to

Maine: the *MICMAC* and several of the *ABENAKI* peoples, the *MALISEET*, *PASSAMAQUODDY*, and *PENOBSCOT*. They joined together in order to make peace with the aggressive Mohawk, an *IROQUOIS* people, and their allies, the Algonquian-speak-ing *OTTAWA*, during a period of strife in 18th century that was fuelled by European political rival-ries and by competition in the fur trade. The western Abenaki, a hor-ticultural people occupying the most southerly part of this region, also joined for a brief time.

WALAM OLUM (*DELAWARE*) is an account of Delaware *CREATION* and migration, painted and en-graved in 183 red pictographic characters on wooden sticks. The authenticity of this artifact has been debated by academics since it was first brought to light by the French scholar Constantine Samuel Rafin-esque in 1836. An analysis of Rafinesque's original papers, un-dertaken in 1998, suggested that he had first written the document in English and then translated it into Delaware.

"ALWAYS RIDING" was a Ute leader of the Yampah band. Federal officials brought Ute leaders to Washington in 1868 for treaty negotiations. The government broke the treaty in 1873 and, within a few years, the Ute had lost most of their remaining lands.

NEW MYTHOLOGIES

NATIVE NORTH AMERICANS must fight to preserve the knowledge and wisdom of their ancestors in a world dominated by Western culture. But thousands of years of adaptation have also taught them to look ahead to the welfare of future generations. Ritual practices once confined to specific tribes and culture areas, such as the sweatlodge and the sundance, have spread across the continent, helping to reinforce the spirits of peoples threatened by extinction. New religions, such as the Native American Church, have rites that seem to resonate with the ancient past, while admitting some elements of Christianity. These groups give strength to native identity and provide a traditional path towards the future. Many other native people are Christians and, although some of

A VISITOR leaves the Clan House at Totem Bight State Park, Ketchikan, Alaska. While the original Northwest Coast villages were almost completely abandoned during the late 19th century, new housebuilding and carving are beginning to revive the ancient crafts.

their churches accommodate traditional beliefs and practices, others resolutely reject non-Christian symbolism, ritual paraphernalia or ceremonies. For all that, the spirits of the earth are alive outside organized religion, since the rich narrative tradition thrives in

AN INUKSUIT, a stone figure constructed by Inuit hunters to drive caribou, stands snow-covered on an Arctic winter day. What was once practical is now sacred, as aboriginal people treasure every surviving trace of their original life, before the coming of white people.

the creative arts. Native artists, dancers, writers and musicians use modern media as a new form of story-telling, one that shows respect for the old and yet gives life to the new. This creative energy is helping to change the face of native culture, yet it is still in keeping with the ancients. Mythology is a way of expressing the rich and wondrous texture of life as it is lived, and so it is appropriate that the old culture heroes live on in new worlds of expression.

OJIBWAY ARTIST (above) Blake Debassige is part of a generation of painters who have followed the lead of Norval Morriseau in translating traditional ideas into a modern idiom. In his surreal Bear Driving a Cadillac (above), Debassige imagines what it would be like if this powerful ancestor lived in the world of modern capitalism.

SIOUX ARTIST (left) Oscar Howe (1915–1983) used the symbols of the circle and Tahokmu, or spider web, to create swirling interplays of colour and form on traditional themes. Woman Scalp Dancer (left) depicts a Sioux ceremony, when enemy scalps were taken for protection from the spirits of those they had killed.

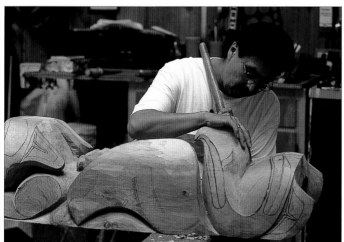

AT BEAR BUTTE (above) western South Dakota, one of the most important sacred places of the Sioux, traditional religion dovetails with tourism, as the site is also a park. Near the sign warning away recreational visitors are prayer flags and bundles left by Native American worshippers.

A TLINGIT CARVER works on a new totem pole at Ketchikan, in southeast Alaska. The great tradition of Northwest Coast art survived the depredations of the historic period and flourishes once again. While it continues to have profound cultural meaning to the tribes along the coast, the outpouring of wood and stone carvings, paintings, prints and jewellery is also recognized as an important part of the world's artistic heritage.

THE WAPPO, speakers of a Yuki language, once lived among the mountains of northern California, hunting small game, fishing and gathering acorns and other wild plants. Like most of the California tribes, the Wappo were either eliminated or forced from their lands by incoming white people, and there were none left in their aboriginal home in the Napa Valley in 1908. The descendants of the surviving Wappo now occupy small landholdings in the region.

WATER SERPENTS are creatures that figure in mythologies across North America.

Among the *HOPI*, Paalölöqangw is both feared and respected. He resembles a giant rattlesnake, with a round, greenish head, protruding eyes, a mouth studded with sharp teeth, a large horn and a crest of ochre-stained feathers. These attributes, resembling those of Quetzalcóatl, the feathered serpent god of the Toltecs and Aztecs, reflect the Mesoamerican influences on Hopi culture. He also sports a fan of eagle tail-feathers and a seashell necklace. He is master of the ocean, and he lives in springs that he creates by vomiting up water. The Hopi pray to him for

THE IMPACT *of the White Man is evident on this Cherokee man's fine ceremonial costume. Along with traditional features – quilled sash, nose ring, long ear loops and earrings – he sports a large silver trade breastplate and a silver medallion.*

THIS SOUTHERN Ojibway ceremonial drumstick is made of an animal jawbone carved in the shape of Mishipizheu, the great horned water serpent who lives in deep lakes and rivers.

rain. In one tradition, the serpent lies across the oceans, with the *TWIN* war gods straddling him, keeping watch over the Hopi. If the people begin to falter in their observance of proper ritual, the twins, along with their grandmother, *SPIDER WOMAN*, will cause the serpent to writhe and drown the entire earth.

The Chiricahua *APACHE* regard some springs as abodes of water monsters, and so they are afraid of using them. In one account, a young girl went to fill her water jar and disappeared. Her mother sought out a *SHAMAN*, who conducted ceremonies for four nights and called in a spirit who told the girl's father to go to the spring. There, the father saw a strange man, with long hair and eyes as bright as the stars, rise out of the water with the daughter at his side. She told him that the man was her husband, and that she now preferred her new underwater home. To compensate her father for his loss, the couple foretold that as long as he stayed in his own country, he would be a great hunter and kill many deer. Unfortunately, he eventually decided to leave his home and his people, and ultimately died in a war with the invading Spanish.

WEEPING WOMAN (*HAIDA*) or Djilákons, is one of the mythic mothers of the Haida moieties, the two halves into which Haida *CLANS* are divided (the other is *FOAM WOMAN*). In one version, she takes the form of a frog whom some hunters have offended. In retaliation, she destroys all humans in a volcanic eruption – except for one girl, who becomes the ancestor of the *EAGLES*. In another version, she gives birth to all the clans herself.

WENEBOJO see *NANABUSH*.

WHITE-BUFFALO-CALF WOMAN (Lakota *SIOUX*) is the great supernatural being who is credited with providing the most powerful tribal *MEDICINE* of the Lakota, the Calf Pipe.

In one account, the Lakota once lived beside a lake far to the east, but, after a hard winter, they were forced to migrate. Two scouts sent ahead suddenly encountered a beautiful maiden dressed in sage, holding a buffalo-skin bundle. One of them rushed at her lustfully, but she brought down rattlesnakes, and he was reduced to bones. She instructed the other to construct a circle of green boughs, and told him she would reappear in front of the entire tribe. Before the people she unwrapped the *PIPE* and instructed them in the songs and prayers of the five great ceremonies: the Foster-parent Chant, the *SUN DANCE*, the Vision Cry, the Buffalo Chant and the Ghost-keeper. She told them that they would always be a nation if they revered the pipe. Then she disappeared, and the people saw only a white buffalo calf on the prairie.

WHITE CLAY PEOPLE see *GROS VENTRE*.

WHITE MAN's first dramatic appearance to the Native Americans is preserved in several oral traditions. The *CHINOOK* tell of the sighting of the first ship. A woman gazed out to sea and saw a strange object that looked like a whale, except that it had two spruce trees standing upright on it. She moved closer and saw that it was clad with copper and had ropes tied to the trees. When a bear came out of this strange object, she saw that it had the face of a human being. Terrified, she ran to the village, crying, and the people rushed back to confront this monster. The two strange men they found there held out copper kettles and put their hands to their mouths, asking for water. After capturing them as slaves, the Chinook burned the vessel.

Oral traditions needed to account for the presence of Europeans in *CREATION*. In two accounts, *COYOTE* is held responsible.

In the *PIMA* version, Coyote pestered the creator as he attempted to fashion human beings out of clay. When the creator went out for wood to fire the clay, Coyote took the clay figures out of the kiln and moulded them into dogs. Now suspicious of Coyote, the creator placed a further batch of clay humans in the kiln and fired them. However, he then foolishly believed it when Coyote told him that the batch was done. The figures turned out pale and underdone: the first white people.

In the *FLATHEAD* version, Old-Man-in-the-Sky, the creator, had to placate *OLD MAN COYOTE* (Coyote as a first being) by creating human companions for him, because he was so lonely that his weeping threatened to cause a new world flood. The creator sent him off to fill a parfleche (rawhide bag) with red earth. Coyote was so tired after filling the bag that he fell asleep. While he slept, Mountain Sheep happened along and decided to trick him. He emptied the bag, filled the bottom with white earth, topped it up with red and put it back. When Coyote finally returned to the creator, it was almost dark. The creator took the soil out of the bag and began to shape two men and two women – the first people – and Coyote took them down to the land and gave them breath. Only in the morning light did he discover that one of the two pairs was white.

A Chiricahua *APACHE* narrative resolves the problem of accounting for the creation of the material culture of Europeans via two *CULTURE HEROES*, *CHILD-OF-THE-WATER* and Killer-of-Enemies (a brother or other relation). The connection is made between Killer-of-Enemies and European culture because he received corn (maize) from Yusn, the creator. Corn and all other domesticated plants and animals, guns and other trade goods are therefore under his purview. Child-of-the-Water is associated with traditional weapons and foods, since he and his mother first collected wild plants.

WHITE-PAINTED WOMAN

(Chiricahua *APACHE*) was mother of the *CULTURE HERO CHILD-OF-THE-WATER*. She supported her child hero and instructed the Chiricahua in the girls' puberty rite and other important ceremonies.

THE WICHITA

, a Caddoan-speaking people, raised corn (maize), beans, squash and other crops in the river basins of the southern Great Plains. They lived in grass-thatched conical huts,

A WINNEBAGO woman weaves a basket using thin splints of oak. Traditional basket designs had names and meanings, often associated with beings and events held sacred by the tribe.

surrounded by their crops. In 1872, they were relocated to reservation lands in Indian Territory (which eventually became Oklahoma); however, the United States Congress never ratified the agreement and, in 1901, most of the original Wichita lands were opened for allotment to white settlers. Today, the tribe controls a mere 4 ha (10 acres), although it shares 972 ha (2,400 acres) with two other tribes, the related Caddo and the *DELAWARE*.

A WICHITA lodge consists of a dome-shaped pole framework, thatched with grass, with a smoke-hole in the centre.

WIDOWER-FROM-ACROSS-THE-OCEAN

see *WOHPEKUMEU*.

WINABOJO see *NANABUSH*.

WÍNDIGO

(northern Algonquians) is a cannibal giant with a heart of ice, a personification of madness associated with either winter starvation or extreme gluttony.

The *OJIBWAY* see the Wíndigo as a giant *MANITOU*, in the form of a man or woman, who is afflicted with a never-ending hunger. This ghastly monster resembles a body removed from a grave – withered, skeletal and with the smell of death. When the Wíndigo prepares to attack a person, a dark snow-cloud rises up, the air turns so cold that the trees crack, and the wind causes a blizzard. The monster tears its victims apart, eating their flesh and bones, and drinking the blood, and some people die of fright when they see it or hear its shriek. Yet, the more the creature eats, the hungrier it gets,

and so it perpetually rages through the dark forests in search of new prey. One lesson of the Wíndigo, therefore, is moderation – it teaches of the need for people to manage critical food supplies so that they can avoid winter famine.

THE WINNEBAGO

[Ho-Chunk] are a Siouan-speaking people who originated in present-day Wisconsin, to the south of the Great Lakes, where they hunted, fished, gathered wild rice, and grew corn (maize) and other crops.

In 1826–7, they rose up against encroaching settlers, and then, in 1840, they were forcibly removed from their homeland to northeast Iowa. In the following decades, they were relocated several times: first to central Minnesota, then to South Dakota and finally, in 1863, to the Winnebago Reservation in northeast Nebraska. During the 1880s, when half of their members moved back to Wisconsin, the Winnebago tribe separated into the two distinct groups that exist today: the original Hochungra ("People of the Big Voices") in Nebraska, and the returnees, the Wonkshieks ("First People of the Old Island"), in Wisconsin.

WINTU, or Wintun, are a small Penutian-speaking northern California people who once hunted and gathered in the Sacramento Valley. They suffered greatly during the invasion by white people, losing their lands and approximately 80 per cent of their population. They retain some small land-holdings, and continue to struggle to keep their traditional way of life.

WISAKEDJAK (Wisaka) (Algonquians, including *KICKAPOO, CREE, FOX,* and *POTAWATOMI*) is in many characteristics analogous to the *OJIBWAY* hero *NANABUSH*.

A Plains *CREE* account begins with a variation of the monstrous *FLYING HEAD* theme. A woman gave birth to two sons, the eldest being Wisakedjak. One day, her husband discovered her consorting with snakes, so he ordered his sons to run away, and in a rage killed the snakes, fed his wife their blood, chopped off her head and fled into the sky. The furious woman sent her buttocks after the boys and her head after the husband. The buttocks caught up with the children at a river, but a crane picked them up and flew them across to safety. The crane then picked up the mother (she was now whole again) and dropped her into the water, where she changed into a sturgeon.

THE WOLVERINE of the mythological age took on the traits of the humans he would harass in the present world. In a Dena tale, Wolverine traps and eats people until he is outwitted by Traveller, the Dena culture hero, who kills the entire family except one wolverine daughter. Her revenge is to make all wolverine thieving and destructive to humans, stealing animals from traps and breaking into caches of meat.

Free from his mother, Wisakedjak left his younger brother and set off on monster-slaying adventures. While he was away, the brother turned into a wolf and was eventually killed by *WATER SERPENTS*, who used his hide as a door flap. On hearing of his brother's fate, Wisakedjak stormed the serpents' den and killed their chief but, in the struggle, the serpents caused a world flood. The hero survived, however, by building a raft, and then sent a loon (great northern diver) down to fetch some earth, and created the world anew.

THE WIYOT, an Algic-speaking culture, once fished, hunted and gathered along the coast of northwestern California. They were almost wiped out by incoming white people, most notably in 1860, when a large ceremonial gathering was massacred by citizens of the town of Eureka – a traumatic event that influences the lives of Wiyot to this day. They now have three small land-holdings (*rancherias*) in the region.

WOHPEKUMEU (*YUROK*), the Widower-From-Across-the-Ocean, is a *CULTURE HERO, TRICKSTER* and *TRANSFORMER* whose various achievements include stealing salmon and acorns for humankind, regulating the rivers and instituting natural childbirth (instead of violent caesarean births).

WOLVERINE, an important *TRICKSTER* and *TRANSFORMER*, may destroy traps and furs like his animal counterpart, but he also has powers of healing.

The *DENA* believe that he made all flint tools by gnawing rocks to shape them. In a parable for children, Wolverine teaches the importance of trust and prudence. Near the beginning of the world, Wolverine stole two children and kept them in a tree cache. In another cache below, he kept his food; there were all sorts of food in

his cache, but he fed the children only fat. One day, the curious children decided to look in Wolverine's cache. When they discovered all the food, they stole some meat and then confronted Wolverine, demanding to know why he kept it to himself. He told them that he had been saving the meat for the future, when they were out on their own – but, because they had betrayed his trust, they would become thieves and liars instead.

WOMAN-WHO-FELL-FROM-THE-SKY (*IROQUOIS*) figures in an explanation of the *CREATION* of the world.

In a land above the sky, a young woman became the bride of an older man but transgressed (in some versions committed adultery), and this caused the tree of life to be uprooted. (In another version, she married a chief and fell ill. In a *DREAM*, the chief was advised to lay her beside the tree that sup-

plied corn [maize] to the people, and to dig it up.) The pregnant woman fell (or was pushed or kicked) through the hole where the tree had been and plummeted towards the water below, but some ducks (or geese) cushioned her descent and held her in the air. Then, to make her a permanent resting place, the assembled animals agreed to create land. Muskrat volunteered to dive under the water for some mud, but he drowned and floated to the surface. Fortunately, Beaver found enough mud in Muskrat's claws and mouth to fashion some land, and Turtle volunteered to support it. The new earth and Turtle grew larger, and the woman gave birth to TWINS, the CULTURE HERO Sapling and his evil contrary, FLINT.

THE WYANDOT

The WYANDOT are the descendants of two Iroquoian tribes, the Huron and the Tobacco, who lived in what is now southern Ontario, between Lake Simcoe and Georgian Bay, on Lake Huron. They were organized in a loose confederacy called the Wendat. The IROQUOIS drove these two horticultural tribes from the region in the middle of the 17th century and scattered them east along the St Lawrence River and south of the Great Lakes. A small number of the Huron eventually settled in Quebec, but the rest of the group escaped to the west end of Lake Erie, where they became known as the Wyandot. In 1843, they were forcibly removed to Kansas, from where most of them were driven out again by 1857 and settled in northeastern Oklahoma.

THE YAKIMA are an amalgam of once-independent tribes and bands, speaking several different languages, who occupied the Plateau region in south-central Washington State. They were predominantly salmon fishers and gatherers along the Columbia River and its tributaries.

After acquiring horses in 1730, they took up buffalo hunting and adopted some cultural traits of Plains tribes. They were forcibly removed to a reservation in the region in 1855, but did retain

THE RECONSTRUCTED Sainte-Marie among the Hurons is a mission founded by French Jesuits in 1639 in the land of the people known then as the Huron (in present-day southern Ontario). In 1649, the Iroquois attacked it in the course of their destruction of the Huron, Tobacco and Neutral tribes, and killed Fathers Jean de Brébeuf and Gabriel Lalemant along with many Wendat. The survivors scattered, and the descendants of one group became the Wyandot Nation of Kansas.

sufficient land (approximately 567,000 ha/1.4 million acres at present) to survive economically and maintain their cultural identity.

YAMANHDEYA (DENE), also known as He-Went-Around-the-Edge, was a CULTURE HERO who travelled around the rim of the earth in his pursuit of monsters. The BEAVER know him as Saya.

YELLOWKNIFE See DENE.

THE YOSEMITE (Sierra Miwok) people are the most southerly of the Sierra MIWOK, and are one of the groups belonging to the Miwok language family. They were hunters and gatherers, and occupied the Sierra Nevada foothills of central California. They suffered the depredations typical of California tribes during white settlement – disease, killing and dislocation – but the tribe nonetheless continues to inhabit small land-holdings within its traditional territory.

THIS YAKIMA BOY (left) wears traditional costume at the Ellenburg Rodeo, Washington State. Pow-wows and rodeos provide Native North Americans with a public outlet for their proud cultures, seen most dramatically in their ceremonial dances.

THE YUKI people are a small northern California hunting and gathering tribe, named after the language they speak, who were almost eliminated during the 19th-century settlement of the region by whites. Along with the MAIDU, WINTU and other aboriginal groups in the area, they were relocated during the 1860s and 1870s on the Round Valley Indian Reservation within traditional Yuki territory. Their language is now extinct, but they maintain their cultural identity.

THE YUROK, an Algonquian people, lived in northwestern California around the mouth of the Klamath River. They subsisted primarily on the abundant salmon, small game and acorns of this area. Having managed to resist white incursions during and after the Gold Rush of 1849, they were forced into the Klamath River Reservation (which ran along 32 km/20 miles of the river) in 1855, and the Hoopa Valley Reservation in 1864. After further land reductions, the tribe now hold approximately 3,645 ha (9,000 acres) of reservation land and allotments.

THE ZUNI people are a Western PUEBLO tribe, speaking a language isolate (unrelated to any known language family) that some linguists classify under the Penutian family. They once occupied the Zuni and Little Colorado River valleys in New Mexico and Arizona. They grow corn (maize) and other crops and, since the coming of Europeans, herd sheep and other animals. Their philosophical organization and their world view are structured on an intricate system of spatial domains, incorporating the seven original villages and the four corresponding cardinal directions plus zenith, nadir and centre. All social, religious and environmental patterns are oriented within this system, managed by an organized priesthood. The Zuni refer to each of their villages as itiwana, meaning "the middle place". The original Zuni reservation was established in 1877, but the United States government reduced this holding substantially in the 20th century. Although they remain in their ancestral lands, and have very successfully resisted the incursions of European and American culture, the Zuni now control less than 3% of their original territory.

A ZUNI MAN stands beside an eagle on its cage. As the eagle is a great hunter and powerful ancestor, its feathers are highly valued in ritual and ceremony by many different tribes.

CHRONOLOGY

ORIGINS
14,000–11,000 BC
The first humans colonized North America during the last ice age, hunting and foraging along ice-free margins of lands connecting Asia and North America. This probably took place after c. 14,000 BC, when the ice sheets began to retreat. Current evidence in southern Chile indicates that humans had reached the tip of South America by at least 10,500 BC.

PALEOINDIANS
10,500–6,000 BC
The first North Americans were nomadic big-game hunters who exploited mammoth, elk, bison and other large Ice Age animals. These groups spread across the continent by c. 9,500 BC.

7000 BC Kennewick Man
Approximately 9,000 years ago, an adult male died along the Columbia River in present-day Washington state. He had a number of injuries, including a projectile point embedded in his pelvis. Anthropologists studying the skeleton found traits more consistent with caucasoids (i.e. peoples originating in Europe, North Africa, and the Middle East to Northern India) than mongoloids (i.e. most of the peoples of East Asia). A struggle between anthropologists and Native American tribal groups continues in the courts for possession of the remains. The cultural affiliation of Kennewick Man remains unresolved.

ARCHAIC HUNTERS AND GATHERERS
6,000–1,000 BC
As humans adapted to the wide range of habitats across the continent, they hunted and gathered an increasing diversity of plants and animals with a wider range of tools and technologies. Evidence of art, religion, and aesthetics begin to appear.

3000–1000 BC Native Copper
Various eastern North American cultures obtained high quality native copper from the Lake Superior region. They heated and hammered the metal to shape tools and ornaments.

2000 BC Pottery
Pottery first appears on the continent in the southeast, along the coasts of Georgia and South Carolina and the coast of Florida.

1550–1050 BC Agriculture
Ancestors of THE PUEBLO peoples in the Southwest begin to grow maize, squash and beans.

1500–600 BC
Poverty Point Culture
A distinctive regional culture in the Lower Mississippi Valley. Unlike neighbouring peoples, this group constructed large earthworks and traded widely for exotic raw materials, such as steatite, copper and haematite.

LATE PREHISTORIC
1000 BC–AD 1500
The introduction of agriculture and pottery caused great change in ways of life across temperate parts of the continent. Food production required a more sedentary lifestyle, which encouraged the development of permanent settlements. The creation of surplus enabled diversification and specialization in technologies. With increasing social complexity, organized political and religious institutions developed.

550 BC–AD 1000 Dorset culture
A distinctive culture of sea-mammal hunters in the eastern and central Canadian Arctic and Greenland. Dorset artists made small ivory carvings of animals and human-like beings, probably for use in ritual activity.

500 BC–AD 400 Adena culture
A hunting and gathering society in the Ohio River basin. The Adena constructed a variety of elaborate ceremonial buildings, earthen enclosures and burial mounds. Their use of a wide range of exotic materials for burial goods, including gold, silver, copper, and shell from the Gulf of Mexico, suggests that they had a class system.

100 BC–AD 1300 Anasazi culture
The Anasazi developed among the canyons and mesas at the present-day intersection of Utah, Colorado, Arizona and New Mexico. About AD 750 they created the pueblo, an above-ground multi-roomed structure made of mud bricks (adobe). They excelled at weaving and ceramics and specialized crafts such as feathered cotton fabrics and turquoise jewellery. Mysteriously, they abandoned their villages, beginning in about AD 1300, and disappeared as a cultural entity.

AD 1–400 Hopewell culture
Hopewell culture developed in the Ohio River basin slightly later than Adena and appears to be an elaboration of the Adena way of life. Hopewell mortuary rituals involved a distinctive symbolism and a range of exotic grave goods, such as headdresses, necklaces, pan pipes, breastplates and oversized display weapons. Hopewell influence extended from the Great Lakes to the Gulf of Mexico and from the central Great Plains to the Atlantic coast.

AD 200–1450 Hohokam culture
The Hohokam farmed along the Gila and Salt Rivers in the Sonoran desert by irrigating their fields. Their use of plazas, ballcourts, and platform mounds shows that Aztec influence. Snaketown, a large Hohokam site on the Gila River in Arizona, had 100 pit houses covering 120 hectares.

AD 700–1600 Mississippian cultures
A rich and elaborate agricultural society developed in the southeast out of Adena and Hopewell cultures. Mississippian peoples grew a wide variety of foods, including maize, beans, squash, pumpkins and tobacco. Their largest town was Cahokia, near present-day St. Louis, Missouri. It had an estimated population of 75,000, housed in large residential areas among more than 100 earthen mounds and plazas.

AD 750–1050 Effigy mound cultures

Hunting and gathering groups in the upper Mississippi Valley known for their distinctive earthen mounds, often in the shape of animals, birds or other non-geometric forms. A site near Harpers Ferry, Iowa, had 895 mounds, 174 of them effigies.

AD 800 Maize becomes the dominant agricultural crop across North America.

AD 800–1525 Athapascan groups begin to migrate south from northern Canada, probably along the eastern edge of the Rocky Mountains, eventually settling in the Southwest. THE APACHE and THE NAVAJO are among several Athapascan-speaking tribes in the region today.

AD 900–1180 Pueblo Bonito

The largest Anasazi pueblo is built, in Chaco Canyon, northwestern New Mexico. It contained approximately 695 rooms, 33 kivas, and 3 great kivas.

AD 900–1250 Thule culture

A sea-mammal hunting culture, ancestral to THE INUIT, begin to move from the Bering Sea region eastward across the Arctic, displacing the Dorset people. The Thule reached Greenland about AD 1250.

AD 900–1350 THE IROQUOIS tribes now known as the Seneca, Cayuga, Onondaga, Oneida, and Mohawk form the original Iroquois Confederacy.

EUROPEAN CONTACT AD 1000–1497

Europeans came to North America long before Christopher Columbus reached the Caribbean and Central America in the late 15th century. In 995–996 Lief Eriksson reached a landfall somewhere along the eastern coast, a place he called Vinland. Thorfinn Karlsefin and Thovald Eriksson followed a similar course and landed near the northern tip of Newfoundland at a place now called L'Anse aux Meadows in c. 998. They settled there for three years. While European fishermen probably exploited the Grand Banks of Newfoundland during the 15th century, the next recorded European presence in North America was John Cabot's voyage to Newfoundland in 1497.

1250–1470 New religious ideas, culminating in the KACHINA cult, spread from the Aztec in Mexico to THE HOPI and eventually to all THE PUEBLO peoples of the Southwest.

1350 The Norse begin to abandon Greenland as the climate grows too cool for agriculture.

1450 The Hokoham abandon their settlements in the Southwest, possibly because of drought.

1492–1504 Christopher Columbus, searching for a western route to Asia, lands in the Bahamas in 1492. In his four voyages to the New World, he explores several islands in the Caribbean and reaches the coast of Panama, but he never sets foot in North America.

1497 John Cabot becomes the first European since the Norse to visit North America, making landfall somewhere on the eastern coast of Newfoundland.

1500 The Arctic climate continues to cool, eventually pushing THE INUIT from the northern Arctic islands and northern Greenland to the northern coastal fringes of North America.

EUROPEAN INVASION 1500–1600

With sea routes to North America established, the European invasion of the continent began. The first Europeans arrived in search of the fabulous riches that a direct sea route to Asia promised. What they found were vast open lands, a wealth of resources, and thriving aboriginal cultures many thousands of years old. Disease, warfare and Christianity eventually uprooted, shattered and decimated all the tribal groups that the colonizers encountered.

1520 Soldiers accompanying the Spanish explorer Cortés had smallpox. As the native population had no resistance to the disease, massive epidemics swept across Mexico and eventually spread into North America. Over the next three hundred years, the disease decimated many tribes. Millions died.

1540 The Spanish explorer Coronado visits Acoma Pueblo, believed to be the oldest inhabited settlement in the US (dates from 12th century). THE ZUNI people see HORSES for the first time.

1570 Europeans begin to explore the coast of Arctic Canada for whale oil, furs and to find new sea routes to Asia.

1585 Sir Walter Raleigh lands on the northeast coast. Disregarding the rights of the native population he claims the land for the English, naming it Virginia.

1607 English colony of Jamestown is established in Virginia.

1622–1646 War between the Jamestown colony and the Powhatan Confederacy.

1629 Spanish Franciscan monks built a fortified mission at Isleta Pueblo, New Mexico.

1632 The Jesuit missionary Paul le Jeune writes the first annual report of missionary work in the New World. These annual Relations, which ceased in 1673, document the Christianizing of tribal people in New France.

1670 Formation of the Hudson's Bay Company to manage the fur trade in the north.

1675–1676 King Philip's war, between the New England colonists and the Wampanoag, Nipmuc, and Narraganset tribes. It ended with the virtual extermination of the tribes.

1680 THE PUEBLO rebellion. The Rio Grande Pueblos rose up against the Spanish, beseiged Santa Fe and drove the colonists back to Mexico. The Pueblo capture of many horses was instrumental in the rapid spread of the horse to native groups across the continent.

1689–1763 The French and Indian Wars, a period of intense rivalry between France and Britain, as they fought for possession of North America.

EUROPEAN CONSOLIDATION 1700–1900

During the 18th and 19th centuries, the British, Spanish and French colonists, and their successors, the nation-states of the United States and Canada, first involved the native peoples in the fur trade and then drove them from their traditional lands to make room for the flood of European immigrants. There were many conflicts. Governments forced tribes to sign treaties, which tended to last only as long as they saw no economic or social benefit in the lands set aside. They also attempted to eliminate all native cultural beliefs and practices by banning traditional languages and religions.

1763 Pontiac, an Ottawa chief, foments rebellion against the English, backed by a confederacy of regional tribes and with the collusion of the French.

1769 Spanish explorer Gaspar de Portola and Father Junipero Serra set up the first of 21 Catholic missions in California.

1778 On March 30th, Captain James Cook and his crew sail into Nootka Sound and first contact the native people of Vancouver Island, on the north Pacific coast.

1778 The United States enacts its first treaty with an Indian nation, THE DELAWARE.

1827 The sac and FOX nations fight to retain the last of their tribal lands. The rebellion ends in 1832 with the massacre of Bad Axe, during which the leader Black Hawk is killed.

1829 The death of the last Beothuk, a young woman named Shawnadithit, from tuberculosis. The Beothuk were the original inhabitants of Newfoundland.

1830 US President Andrew Jackson signs the Indian Removal Act, designed to eliminate all native settlement east of the Mississippi River. THE CHEROKEE appealed this ruling successfully in the Supreme Court, but Jackson ignored the ruling and the government enacted the plan with the collusion of the states.

1831–1839 The Trails of Tears, harsh and illegal removal by the US government of the Five Civilized Tribes (THE CHEROKEE, CHOCTAW, CREEK, Chickasaw, SEMINOLE) in forced marches from their lands in the Southeast to Oklahoma, with heavy loss of life.

1835–1858 The Seminole Wars, resistance by THE SEMINOLE to their removal from traditional lands in Florida. Most were eventually relocated in Oklahoma, but at least two hundred resisted successfully and their descendants remain in Florida today. The Seminoles never surrendered and have no peace treaty with the United States government.

1849 Onset of the gold rush in California, which precipitated the wholesale massacre of Indian populations.

1868 The US government signed a treaty with the Sioux tribes of the Dakota territory, creating the Great Sioux Reservation, which included the Black Hills. The government violated the treaty and confiscated the land in 1877 soon after they discovered gold.

1876 Battle of Little Big Horn between the US Army's Seventh Cavalry, commanded by General George Armstrong Custer, and Lakota, CHEYENNE and ARAPAHO warriors. Custer and his men were wiped out.

1880–1890 Gold rush in Alaska and the Yukon leads to the mass settlement of the western Arctic.

1887 The Dawes Act, a scheme to break up reservation lands and assimilate Indian people, was enacted. The plan was to lure tribal people into accepting individual allotments of 160 acres in return for their collective treaty rights.

1889 The Oklahoma Land Rush, a race among prospective white settlers for land taken from the territory granted previously to the native tribes after the Indian Removal Act of 1830.

1890 The US 7th Cavalry massacred a band of Lakota SIOUX men, women and children they had captured at Wounded Knee Creek, on the Pine Ridge Reservation in Dakota Territory.

1891 The Act for the Relief of the Mission Indians. After more than a hundred years of attempted extermination of the California Indian tribes, this act set aside small reservations for surviving tribal people.

1900–PRESENT

By the end of the 19th century, the entire aboriginal population of the New World was either confined to land reserves or managed within the vast forests and tundra of the Arctic and sub-Arctic. Reservations in the United States often threw together tribes with distinct languages and cultural traditions, and governments continued to try to assimilate all of these captive populations by encouraging missionary activity and making Western education compulsory. These efforts seriously damaged or destroyed thousands of years of culture, but many tribes managed to keep their traditions alive.

1924 The US Congress passed the Citizenship Act, designed to confer citizenship on Native Americans and hasten their assimilation. Several states did not grant Indian people the right to vote.

RENEWAL

1934 The Indian Reorganization Act replaces the Dawes Act of 1887. It recognizes the rights of native people to hold land and ends the official sanction of assimilation.

1944 The National Congress of American Indians is established in the United States.

1946 Indian Claims Commission set up to negotiate regarding illegally lost lands and resources.

1965 Last known speaker of CHUMASH (Hokan family) dies.

1968 Founding of the American Indian Movement (AIM), a radical organization which is dedicated to the fight for Native American rights.

1973 Siege at Wounded Knee, an occupation of lands in Pine Ridge Reservation by AIM supporters. A violent stand-off with the FBI ended after 71 days.

1978 The American Indian Freedom of Religion Act recognizes the constitutional right of native people in the US to practice their own religions.

1990 Native American Graves Protection and Repatriation Act recognizes that prehistoric and historic native burials, burial sites and associated artefacts are the property of tribes.

1999 Canada establishes Nunavut ("our land") as an Inuit homeland. The new territory consists of the central and eastern portions of the Northwest Territories and a majority of Inuit citizens.

2002 Native American Sacred Sites Protection Act tabled in the US Congress.

BIBLIOGRAPHY

Alexander, Hartley Burr (1969) *The World's Rim; Great Mysteries of the North American Indians.* University of Nebraska Press.

Asatchaq (1992) *The Things That Were Said of Them: Shaman Stories and Oral Histories of the Tikigaq People* (transl. by Tukum-miq and Tom Lowenstein). University of California Press.

Bahr, Donald (1994) *The Short, Swift Time of Gods on Earth: The Hohokam Chronicles.* University of California Press.

Barnouw, Victor (1977) *Wisconsin Chippewa Myths and Tales and Their Relation to Chippewa Life.* University of Wisconsin Press.

Bierhorst, John (1985) *The Mythology of North America.* Morrow, NY.

Boas, Franz (1969) *The Religion of the Kwakiutl Indians.* AMS Press, NY.

Boas, Franz (1970) *Tsimshian Mythology.* Johnson Reprint Corp, New York.

Burland, Cottie Arthur (1968) *North American Indian Mythology.* Hamlyn, UK.

Callicott, J. Baird and Overholt, Thomas W. (1982) *Clothed-in-fur, and Other Tales: An Introduction to an Ojibwa World View.* University Press of America, Washington, DC.

Clark, Ella Elizabeth (1966) *Indian Legends from the Northern Rockies.* University of Oklahoma Press.

Coffin, Tristram Potter (1961) *Indian Tales of North America; An Anthology for the Adult Reader.* American Folklore Society, Philadelphia.

Coleman, Bernard, Sister (1971) *Ojibwa Myths and Legends.* Ross and Haines, Minneapolis.

Courlander, Harold (1982) *Hopi Voices: Recollections, Traditions, and Narratives of the Hopi Indians.* University of New Mexico Press.

Davis, Mary B. (ed.) (1994) *Native America in the 20th Century: An Encyclopedia.* Garland. New York.

de Laguna, Frederica (ed.) (1995) *Tales from the Dena: Indian Stories from the Tanana, Koyukuk, and Yukon Rivers.* University of Washington Press.

Dorsey, George Amos (1903) *Traditions of the Arapaho.* Chicago.

Dorsey, George Amos (1904) *Traditions of the Arikara.* The Carnegie Institution of Washington.

Dorsey, George Amos (1904) *The Mythology of the Wichita.* Carnegie Institution of Washington.

Dorsey, George Amos (1969) *Traditions of the Skidi Pawnee.* Kraus Reprint, NY.

Edmonds, Margot (1989) *Voices of the Winds: Native American Legends.* Facts on File, New York.

Erdoes, Richard and Ortiz, Alfonso (eds.) (1984) *American Indian Myths and Legends.* Pantheon Books, New York.

Gill, Sam D. (1992) *Dictionary of Native American Mythology.* Santa Barbara, California.

Grinnell, George Bird (1892) *Blackfoot Lodge Tales; The Story of a Prairie People.* Scribner's Sons, New York.

Highwater, Jamake (1977) *Ritual of the Wind: North American Indian Ceremonies, Music, and Dances.* Viking Press, New York.

Hitakonanulaxk (Tree Beard) (1994) *The Grandfathers Speak: Native American Folk Tales of the Lenape People.* Interlink Books, New York.

Howard, James Henri (1984) *Oklahoma Seminoles: Medicines, Magic, and Religion.* University of Oklahoma Press.

Hultkrantz, Ake (1981) *Belief and Worship in Native North America.* Syracuse University Press, NY

Johnston, Basil (1995) *The Manitous: The Spiritual World of the Ojibway.* HarperCollins, New York.

Josephy, Jr., Alvin (1991) *America in 1492: The World of the Indian Peoples Before the Arrival of Columbus.* Knopf, New York.

Judson, Katharine Berry (1911) *Myths and Legends of Alaska.* A.C. McClurg & Co., Chicago.

Kroeber, Alfred Louis (1978) *Yurok Myths.* University of California Press.

Kroeber, A.L., E.W. Gifford (comp.) (1980) *Karok Myths.* University of California Press.

LaPointe, James (1976) *Legends of the Lakota.* Indian Historian Press, San Francisco.

Leeming, David Adams (1998) *The Mythology of Native North America.* University of Oklahoma Press.

Levy, Jerrold E. (1998) *In the Beginning: The Navajo Genesis.* University of California Press.

Lomatuway'ma, Michael (1993) *Hopi Ruin Legends: Kiqotutuwutsi.* Published for Northern Arizona University by the University of Nebraska Press.

Lowie, Robert Harry (1975) *The Assiniboine.* AMS Press, NY.

Lowie, Robert Harry (1976) *The Religion of the Crow Indians.* AMS Press, New York.

Marriott, Alice Lee (1968) *American Indian Mythology.* Crowell, New York.

Merkur, Daniel (1991) *Powers Which We Do Not Know: The Gods and Spirits of the Inuit.* University of Idaho Press.

Molyneaux, Brian Leigh (1995) *The Sacred Earth.* Macmillan, London.

Opler, Morris Edward (1942) *Myths and Tales of the Chiricahua Apache Indians.* NY.

Penn, W.S. (ed.) (1996) *The Telling of the World: Native American Stories and Art.* Stewart, Tabori & Chang, New York.

Radin, Paul (1948) *Winnebago Hero Cycles: A Study in Aboriginal Literature.* Waverly Press, Baltimore.

Ridington, Robin (1988) *Trail to Heaven: Knowledge and Narrative in a Northern Native Community.* University of Iowa Press.

Schoolcraft, Henry Rowe (1980) *Legends of the American Indians.* Crescent Books, New York.

Shipley, William (ed. and transl.) (1991) *The Maidu Indian Myths and Stories of Hanc'ibyjim.* Heydey Books in conjunction with Rick Heide, Berkeley, CA.

Smith, Anne M. (coll.) (1992) *Ute Tales.* University of Utah Press.

Smith, Theresa S. (1995) *The Island the Anishnaabeg: Thunderers and Water Monsters in the Traditional Ojibwe Life-world.* University of Idaho Press.

Thompson, Stith (1967) *Tales of the North American Indians.* Indiana University Press.

Trafzer, Clifford E. (ed.) (1996) *Blue Dawn, Red Earth: New Native American Storytellers.* Anchor Books, New York.

Waldman, Carl (1985) *Atlas of the North American Indian.* Facts on File, NY.

Williamson, Ray A. (1984) *Living the Sky: The Cosmos of the American Indian.* Houghton Mifflin, Boston.

Williamson, Ray A. and Farrer, Claire R. (eds.) (1992) *Earth and Sky: Visions of the Cosmos in Native American Folklore.* University of New Mexico Press.

Zimmerman, Larry and Molyneaux, Brian Leigh (1996) *Native North America.* Macmillan, London. (Repub. 2000): University of Oklahoma Press.

GENERAL READING

Brotherston, Gordon (1979) *Image of the New World: The American Continent Portrayed in Native Texts.* Thames and Hudson, London and New York.

Coe, Michael, Dean Snow and Elizabeth Benson (1986) *Atlas of Ancient America.* Facts on File, New York and Oxford.

Willis, Roy (ed.), *World Mythology: An Illustrated Guide.* Duncan Baird, London.

PICTURE ACKNOWLEDGEMENTS

The publishers are grateful to the agencies, museums and galleries listed below for kind permission to reproduce the following images in this book:

AKG: 25br; 62br

Brian and Cherry Alexander: 79bl; 84tr; 84bl; 85bl

Art Resource: 21br National Museum of American Art, Washington, DC; 52br; 54tc, 77tr National Museum of American Art, Washington, DC

Artemis Picture Research: 24br

Bancroft Hunt: 19bl; 21tc; 28tr; 28bl; 35tl; 36tr; 42tr; 42bl; 43cr; 46bc; 47tl; 48tl; 48bc; 50tl; 55tr; 55tl; 57bc; 62tc; 63tr; 63bc; 68bc; 69tc; 75tl; 83tl; 86c; 86cl; 87bl; 89br

Bridgeman Art Library: 29tr Library of Congress, Washington, DC; 30br Princeton Museum of Natural History, New Jersey; 65t Royal Ontario Museum, Toronto; 65cr Private Collection; 75br Private Collection

Bruce Coleman: 14tl; 27tl; 31t; 36br; 43bl; 59t; 85br; 88bl

Sylvia Cordaiy: 18br; 20tc; 33br; 59bl; 89tc

Ecoscene: 22b; 37br; 40br; 49tl; 51br

Mary Evans Picture Library: 37bl; 43tc

Favell Museum, Klamath Falls, Oregon: 67tr

Galaxy Picture Library: 27br; 31bl; 64br; 69br; 70bl; 77bl

Gibson Photo: 38c; 38bl; 39t; 39c; 39b

The Granger Collection: 53tl; 72bl; 73tl

Michael Heron: 15tr

Indian and Northern Affairs, Canada: 25c

Brian L. Molyneaux: 31br; 43cl; 43br; 66ct; 73bl; 79t

Peter Newark Pictures: 19tr; 23tc; 46tl; 47cr; 49cr; 49bc; 53cr; 65bl; 70tr; 73cr; 73br; 74tl; 76ct; 78br; 82tl; 83br; 85tr; 89bl

North Wind Pictures: 23cr; 26tr; 29bl; 32br; 36tl; 45tl; 50tr; 50bc; 53cl; 67br; 71ct

Phoebe Hearst Museum of Anthropology, University of California: 53b

Prema Photos: 68tr

Rochester Museum and Science Center: 72tr; 88tr

Santa Barbara Mission Archive-Library: 13br

Smithsonian Institution, Department of Anthropology: 61br

Smithsonian Institution, National Museum of the American Indian: 61tl

Superstock: 26br; 60tl National Museum of Natural History, Smithsonian Institution, Washington, DC; 71br Lowe Art Museum, University of Miami

Travel Ink: 20br; 26cl; 34tr; 40tc; 65br

VBC Museum of Anthropology: 15bl

Werner Forman Archive: 18tc Sheldon Jackson Museum, Alaska; 22tr, 25t, 35br Provincial Museum, Victoria, British Columbia; 37tr National Museum, Denmark; 41tc Arizona State Museum; 44cr; 44bl; 45cr; 51tl Museum of Anthropology, University of British Columbia, Vancouver; 57tr Provincial Museum, Victoria, British Columbia; 60bc Schindler Collection, New York; 74br Field Museum of Natural History, Chicago; 76cl; 79br Haffenreffer Museum of Anthropology, Brown University, Rhode Island; 80tl; 80br; 81tl Provincial Museum, Victoria, British Columbia; 81br; 82br Provincial Museum, Victoria, British Columbia

INDEX

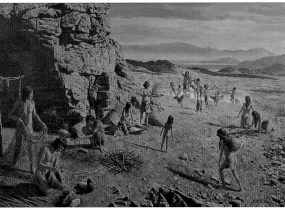
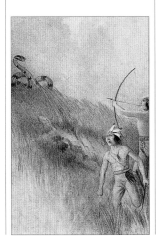